THE RIGHT MAN

"The man I pick has got to be expert enough at covert operations and concealment to be able to get in and out of there undetected."

"Yes sir."

"And he's got to be expert enough at sentry removal and hand-to-hand combat to handle any unpleasantness that might come up."

"Yes sir."

"And he's got to be brave enough and tough enough to do the job."

"Yes sir."

"And one more thing."

"What's that sir?"

"He's got to be crazy enough to try it . . ."

THE SCORPION SQUAD series from Pinnacle Books

THE SCORPION SQUAD

THE NHU KY STING
Eric Helm

PINNACLE BOOKS NEW YORK

This is a work of fiction. All the characters and events portrayed in this book are fictional, and any resemblance to real people or incidents is purely coincidental.

THE SCORPION SQUAD #2: THE NHU KY STING

An original Pinnacle Books edition, published for the first time anywhere.

First printing/November 1984

ISBN: 0-523-42291-1

Can. ISBN: 0-523-43295-X

Cover art by Bruce Minney

Printed in the United States of America

PINNACLE BOOKS, INC.
1430 Broadway
New York, New York 10018

9 8 7 6 5 4 3 2 1

THE NHU KY STING

PROLOGUE_____

Major Malcolm Forbes Jessup leaned back against the air force emergency parachute that served as the only cushion between his pressure-suited spine and the cold, hard surface of his armored ejection seat, and breathed a ragged sigh of relief.

The mission hadn't been a particularly rough one, but it had been nearly seven and a half hours since he'd climbed into the cockpit of the U-2 high altitude reconnaissance jet at Badaber Air Force Base in Pakistan, and the operational details of flying the spy plane at better than 75,000 feet for an extended period of time were both mentally and physically draining. Jessup figured he'd probably lost ten pounds of body weight in sweat alone. The overly sweet odor that floated up into his helmet from down below in the pressure suit—despite the steady stream of pure oxygen washing over his face from the aircraft's life support system—sure smelled like it.

Jessup was looking forward to a long soak in a hot

bath, a snifter of good brandy, and one of those delightful, pre-Castro cigars his father kept sending him from Washington. And the flight surgeon could just try aerial intercourse with a revolving pastry if he didn't like it. One was entitled to enjoy the pleasures of life, especially after a mission this long. Moments of useful consciousness at extreme altitude and retinal-aldehyde deterioration be damned!

The mission profile for the flight had included the routine bi-weekly reconnaissance of the Chinese nuclear experimentation and test facility at Lop Nor, but this time with an added twist. Instead of the normal route—over the Soviet facility in Tashkent to see what Ivan the Terrible was up to, then on to Turkey—he had been instructed to fly southeast. Apparently rumors had drifted back to headquarters at Langley about some unusual activity near a modest-sized city called Gui-yang in southeastern China. Whatever was going on, Langley thought it might be nice to have some pictures, so that Photo-Intell could study them and try to decide if the activity was really unusual. Jessup thought the whole business was rather silly and sounded dreadfully boring.

The only inconvenience was that because of the distance, he'd be landing at Saigon's Ton Son Nhut airport instead of going to Turkey or back to Pakistan. The initial plan had been to land at Udorn, Thailand, but that had been scrapped for some reason or other. Jessup couldn't remember why now. So he was finally going to get an opportunity to visit the Paris of the East. He supposed everyone ought to do that once in his career. The problem was, they had this bothersome little war going on there. It wasn't that he was concerned about actually becoming involved in it. The altitude the U-2 normally operated at put him well above the range of even the Russian air defense missiles and fighter-interceptors. He just hoped some inconsiderate Viet Cong terrorist bomber wouldn't mess up his four-day weekend in Saigon.

So Jessup relaxed when he crossed the Chinese border, heading south into North Vietnam. The job was ended. He'd flown the mission and taken the photos, and was now out of range of the ADA missile sites of the People's Liberation Army. The U-2 was cruising along faultlessly at 590 mph, and Jessup had even descended to 65,000 feet, still well above the ceiling of any missiles, but safer for the mechanics of the aircraft.

In the rarified air at high altitude, a flame-out of the turbojet engine that powered the U-2 was always a possibility. Jessup had experienced several in the past. Although serious, they were rarely a critical problem. A restart could usually be effected at lower altitude, and the glide ratio of the U-2 was phenomenal. The condition was worrisome because it could force you down to where the missiles could get at you, but if you had that kind of problem, it was time to be running for a friendly border and staying the hell away from communist SAM sites. North Vietnam was known to have been supplied with a few SA-2 Guideline missiles by the Soviet Union, but they couldn't have all that many of them. They were probably all deployed around Hanoi and Haipong, and he'd be diverting just a bit to stay well away from those areas. His course would take him just west of an insignificant backwater named Son Tay.

After that, it was a milk run. His flight path wouldn't take him over anything bigger or more sophisticated than a rice paddy. He'd cut a corner off Laos, slice a piece off Cambodia, and be in Saigon, by late afternoon, getting a drink and a bath and deciding which restaurant or nightclub to have dinner in.

Jessup glanced at his Rolex chronometer and smiled.

Hell, he thought. At this rate, I'll be pumping it to some high-class, half-French Vietnamese bitch by 2100 hours. She's got to be half French, though. That's important. Father could understand that. If he ever found out I'd been screwing some common dink, he'd cut me out of his will. That wouldn't do at all, so I'll have to find one who's half French. Shouldn't be all that hard to do in Saigon. Hell, maybe I'll just buy myself two of them. I can afford it. Wouldn't that be something? Four days and four nights, with two of them. They've got to be half French though.

Jessup's plans for an extended weekend of Eurasian libidinal bliss was abruptly terminated by a loud thump from the rear of the aircraft. The U-2 reared up like a stallion, the nose broke over violently to the right in a vicious hammerhead, and the aircraft slipped promptly into a dangerous, flat spin.

Jessup didn't have time to wonder about what he'd hit or been hit by. He shouldn't have hit anything. At 65,000 feet, he'd been too high up for missiles, let alone birds, but the only thing he could think of was that something had struck the aircraft. And now he was in a flat spin, with a howling in his earphones and a control panel full of flashing red lights that told him the sudden pitching of the airplane had caused a compressor stall and resulted in a flame-out.

And right now, the flame-out was the least of his worries. He had a lot of altitude. He could probably restart the engine at a lower altitude, where the air was more dense, if the compressor blades hadn't been damaged. Even if he couldn't, the glide ratio* of the U-2 was so great he could probably make it all the way to Saigon without the engine, starting from 65,000 feet altitude.

The problem was that he wasn't going to be starting a long glide from 65,000 feet. In a flat spin, the U-2 had all the aerodynamic characteristics of a bowling ball. He was losing altitude at an alarming rate. His speed of descent was rapidly increasing, and that, combined with the G-forces created by the spin itself, was putting a tremendous shear load on the U-2's delicate wings. Modeled after the wing structure of sailplanes, the long, slender wings of the aircraft were, paradoxically, both highly flexible and fragile. If Jessup couldn't bring the airplane out of the spin soon, there was a very real possibility that the stress loads being built up on the wings would snap them off like matchsticks. If that happened, he wouldn't have to worry about minor considerations like midair restarts or glide ratios or spending a long weekend with two, half-French Vietnamese prostitutes.

There's a certain humor here, thought Jessup as he struggled with the controls. You're not supposed to be able to pull out of a flat spin without power, and I can't get a smooth enough airflow through the in-

*A glossary appears on page 214.

takes to get a restart while I'm spinning. If this is God's idea of a joke, we are not amused.

Sweat stung Jessup's eyes, yet he felt curiously cold. His world seemed suddenly to have grown small. In all the earth, there was at that moment only the crazily tumbling gyro horizon, the stubbornly flashing engine alarm lights that refused to go out, and the madly unwinding altimeter, cranking inexorably toward zero. He hardly noticed the kaleidoscopic panorama of farmland and sky slashing past the windscreen of the canopy every second and a half.

The altimeter had spun down past 27,000 feet, and Jessup was beginning to feel just a bit queasy from all the revolutions when he finally decided that discretion might be the better part of valor, or at least of flying. Suddenly, running across the North Vietnamese countryside pursued by some NVA patrol really seemed to be preferable to becoming a permanent fixture of it. He was groping for the canopy release when the aircraft lurched sickeningly to the accompaniment of a loud creaking noise in the airframe and popped out of the spin in a steep dive.

Mindful of the protesting metal framework, Jessup did not haul back sharply on the stick, but eased back on it slowly. Hesitantly at first, then more quickly, the nose bobbed up, broke through the horizon, and he had to lower it again to achieve a level flight altitude. He trimmed the aircraft into a shallow glide and took stock of the situation.

He was somewhere immediately southwest of Son Tay, at an altitude of 26,000 feet. He still couldn't get the engine to restart, and he'd suffered impact and structural damage to the aircraft, extent unknown.

For the moment, however, the aircraft was still in one piece and responding to control.

Jessup made a few rapid calculations on his E-6B computer. If he could maximize his glide ratio, there was still a small chance he could make it to Saigon, or at least, Da Nang. Da Nang would be a piece of cake. If the aircraft held together. If he didn't run into any NVAF interceptors. If he didn't accidently overfly some NVA anti-aircraft battery. If his luck held out. If, if, if.

If you're walking on eggs, it isn't smart to play hopscotch.

Jessup didn't have any choice. Another warning light was insistently winking away at him from the flat little black box set atop the left edge of the instrument panel, and a low, angry growl was building up in his earphones now that he'd killed the audible on the engine warning alarm. The noise, and the light, indicated that the small, streamlined ECM pod slung under the left wing of the U-2 had detected an E-band Fan Song radar in operation. Jessup knew that he was being tracked by the Russian-built radar, and that it was used for only one thing: target acquisition for the SAM-2 intermediate and high altitude anti-aircraft missile.

Jessup could see two dirty white contrails arching up toward his aircraft from the rolling countryside far below. Without power, he couldn't outclimb the missiles, and from this height, there wouldn't have been time anyway. He knew, however, that the SAM-2s were slow-turning missiles. If he could pass closely enough to one of them without being blown up, he might be able to slip by it. That would leave only one missile to worry about. Plus any low altitude missiles or anti-aircraft guns whose range the maneuver might force him into. All he could do was hope the ECM package would do its job.

Jessup leaned forward and threw the switch that triggered the E/F band radar-jamming apparatus.

Nothing happened.

He tried again.

Still nothing.

Acting calmly but quickly, he checked the circuit breaker for the jamming box.

It was gone, probably knocked loose somehow during the spin.

Fighting down a sinking feeling in the pit of his stomach and the acrid taste of rising bile at the back of his mouth, Jessup pulled out the circuit breaker for the landing light and shoved it into the clip for the jammer. The set came on, but was slow to warm. From his own radar, and visually, Jessup could tell that the first missile was already dangerously close. Perhaps too close.

"Shit," he said, as he banked the U-2 over into a steep diving turn toward the nearest missile and silently prayed the wings on. "This mess is really going to screw up my weekend in Saigon."

CHAPTER 1 _____

They watched Brigadier General Billy Joe Crinshaw's helicopter disappear in the distance, leaving them standing amid the smoking ruins of Camp A-555. A hundred fires had destroyed most of it and a dozen still burned. Dead bodies—NVA, VC, and South Vietnamese—littered the ground in the camp, near the walls, and in the rice paddies outside. Captain Mack Gerber, the Special Forces A-team commander, didn't know how many had been killed, but guessed that there had to be nearly a thousand dead. On both sides.

When the general's helicopter was gone, Lieutenant Colonel Alan Bates turned to face Gerber and said, ''I guess that takes care of him for a while. He should be content to sit in his office reflecting on our great victory.''

Gerber looked at the ruins of his camp, a camp that the night before had been nearly completed, but still under construction, and now was little more than smoking remains. "I suppose you call it a victory because we still hold it."

Bates took Gerber's elbow and tried to steer him toward the skeleton of the team house to get him away from the other Green Berets who were checking the enemy bodies for weapons, boobytraps, and signs of life. And to get him away from the Vietnamese who were not doing much of anything during the moments of shock after the close of a large-scale fight.

"I call it a victory because the VC failed to take this away from us. Yes, a victory. But don't confuse my attitude with Crinshaw's let-the-newsboys-get-their-story attitude. I know what you're thinking. Unfortunately, it can't be."

Near the team house, they stopped. Gerber stared at Bates, as if seeing him for the first time. "What's that supposed to mean?"

Bates took a deep breath and sighed. "This isn't the time or the place to discuss it."

"Let's make it the time and place," responded Gerber, ignoring the fact that Bates outranked him.

"All right, Mack. Please take this in the spirit in which I say it. But you know I have to bring a new A-team in here. I have no choice."

"Crinshaw tell you that?"

"Crinshaw had nothing to do with it. It's my decision. I didn't say anything while Crinshaw was here because I didn't want him to know, at least yet, that I have to replace you."

For a moment, Gerber's mind spun as if he couldn't understand the meaning of the words. Then, almost as an alibi, he said. "But we held."

"Yes, you did. By the skin of your teeth. But you

did a hell of a job and you'll all be rewarded for that.''

"Then why replace us?"

"Use your head, man. You don't have a team left. You just told me not twenty minutes ago that your executive officer will need to go to Saigon for treatment. We've already evacked a couple of your people, not to mention Cavanaugh, who was in Saigon when this mess began. You've barely got half a team."

"But that's no—"

"Mack, this is not a reflection on you or your team. You people did a hell of a job. But I've got to get a full team in here quickly. Before Crinshaw realizes how badly beat up you are and orders this camp closed. A full team to begin rebuilding while you and your people take a well deserved R and R."

"We don't need an R and R."

"Be reasonable, Mack. We can't leave things the way they are, as much as you or I might want to. I'm not saying this change is permanent. It's something that has to be done now, before Crinshaw decides to take everyone out of here. We snowed him earlier, but that doesn't mean that he won't change his mind."

"We can manage," Gerber protested. "We just need to get some replacement strikers. Lieutenant Bromhead will be back in a couple of days, as will some of the others. We should be at nearly full strength in less than a week. Two at the most."

"There's not much more to—"

The sudden snap of a rifle shot stopped him. He looked to the left and then down at Gerber, who had hit the ground as the round struck the wall between them. Gerber had his rifle pointed toward the sound and was scanning the dead, looking for the imposter.

There was a long burst from a submachine gun. Seeing the bullets hitting the ground around a khaki-clad figure, Gerber leaped to his feet and ran toward the shooting in a low crouch. He got there as two of his team and a dozen Vietnamese were surrounding the bullet-riddled body.

Master Sergeant Anthony Fetterman watched his captain run up and said, "Playing possum. Tried to shoot Colonel Bates, I think. Probably was waiting here for a good target."

"Why didn't he try for Crinshaw or one of the newsmen?"

"Probably figured the colonel for the most valuable target." Fetterman shrugged. "I would imagine that he had been unconscious. Looked like he'd been shot up pretty good in the attack last night."

"Okay," said Gerber angrily. "I want all the fucking weapons picked up, and I mean now. And I want these bodies cleared out of here as quickly as possible. Aside from the disease risk, I don't want another suicidal VC shooting someone now that the real threat is over."

"Yes sir," said Fetterman. "We're working on it."

Gerber shot Fetterman a sharp glance. "I know you are. It's been a long night and I don't see an end in sight." To Bates, who had run up, he said, "How about getting some help in here, at least for today? Evac the bodies of the dead strikers and help us either bury or burn the bodies of the VC."

"I'll tell you what," said Bates. "I'll bring in a

whole new A-team today. You and your men can brief them this afternoon and then be on a chopper tomorrow. I'll see you in Saigon and we can arrange for your R and Rs. Once things are a little more stabilized, you can come back out here.''

Gerber stared at Bates, looking deep into the eyes. He saw that there was no way he was going to avoid this. Rather than arguing anymore, he said stiffly, ''Yes sir,'' then moved off to begin supervising the clean up details.

Just as the sun began to set, the helicopter bringing the new A-team appeared in the distance. Gerber cursed under his breath because it was possibly the worst time that it could come. If there were any VC in the area—and even after the beating the night before there had to be some around—the chopper would provide them with a prime target.

Gerber reminded Fetterman of the alert orders. No one was to be moving around from a half hour before sundown until a half hour after. While Fetterman checked to make sure the alert orders were followed, Gerber and Sergeant Galvin Bocker, the senior communications NCO, went to the helipad to wait for the chopper. Most of the bodies had been moved to the south side of the camp for disposal.

When the helicopter was only a minute out, Gerber threw a smoke grenade to guide it in. There was no fire received and no evidence of enemy action.

The helicopter, an army aviation CH-47 Chinook, kicked up a dust storm that obscured everything as it touched down. The back ramp dropped and two men sprinted out. One of them ran to Gerber.

"Sorry we're late Captain. We'll get our gear out so that the chopper can take off. Then we can talk."

With the Chinook gone, Gerber and Bocker led the new A-team toward the remains of the team house. Over his shoulder Gerber said, "I'm afraid that the team house was pretty well ruined. The frame was fairly sturdy so we've pitched a tent over the top for temporary protection. You can store your gear in there."

Inside there was a Coleman lantern burning, giving off enough light to see. Gerber said, "Put your gear anywhere. You can get it stored later. Right now, Captain, we need to take a look at the camp. I'm afraid that it's in terrible shape. A company could probably take it now. If Charlie has one. But I don't think he has."

Then, as if he had just remembered, he said, "I'm Mack Gerber. That," he said, pointing to a man in the corner, "is Sergeant Bocker, our communications NCO. You might want to have your commo people get with him."

The new captain said, "I'm Dave Henderson. And my XO is Thomas Orwell. Team sergeant is Jesse Bowman."

Gerber nodded and said, "Our team sergeant is Fetterman. He's out right now, checking on the Vietnamese. We'll get you all briefed after we grab a bite to eat. After a look at the overall situation, we can break into small groups and each man can meet with his counterpart to get this ironed out. Well, mostly, anyway. Some of the team has already been medevacked out."

Bocker, taking Gerber's words as a hint, moved to one side of the tent and began pulling out boxes of C-rations. He didn't bother to look at the individual contents of the meals, combat, one each. He just handed the boxes to the new arrivals and said, "Afraid that the bad guys blew up our stove. It's the best we can offer tonight."

Henderson took his and said, "No problem, Sarge. We certainly understand."

"I've got to check things outside," said Gerber. "See you in about tweny minutes."

Before he could get out the door, Henderson said, "Look, I'm sorry about this. I want you—"

"Don't worry about it," said Gerber, breaking in. "I know. It's not your fault."

After the evening alert, Gerber told Fetterman to rotate the guard on two-hour shifts but to keep only about a fifth of the men on alert. Nearly everyone in the camp had been awake for over twenty-four hours and it would be impossible for them to have a full alert during the night, work the next day, and do it all over. They had to get some sleep.

"Besides," Gerber told him, "we can keep all the Americans awake tonight. You guys will be dragging tomorrow, but we're being pulled out so that won't matter. The new guys should be fairly well rested."

"I'll see to it, Captain," said Fetterman. He hesitated, and then made an uncharacteristic remark. "Will we be able to keep the team together?"

Gerber unconsciously raised an eyebrow and studied his short, wiry team sergeant. "I think so. Most of the wounds are minor and shouldn't require a lot of recuperation. Besides, we have enough here to form a solid nucleus. Yeah, I think we can keep the team together. Providing we don't run into another load of shit.''

"That's good, sir. I told Mrs. Fetterman and the kids about you guys and she thinks you'll do everything you can to see that I arrive home healthy.''

The combined meeting went well. Gerber outlined the holes in the defenses that had resulted from the attack. The fire control tower was down, many of the bunkers had been destroyed or heavily damaged, and most of the camp's wooden structures had burned. The runway was full of holes from mortars. There were only a couple of the heavy weapons that hadn't been damaged and there was very little ammunition for them. All the claymores had been used. The only exceptions to the bad news were that the commo bunker was intact, as was most of the north wall and the secondary command bunker.

"The real good news," added Gerber dryly, "is that we could outfit an NVA regiment with the weapons and equipment we've captured. I don't know what we'll do with it all, but I'm sure that some kind of plan will evolve.''

Gerber and the remainder of his team answered questions, and then he watched as the team broke into small groups to go over specifics. He didn't like leaving a new man with this. It was his responsibility to rebuild the camp, not Henderson's. He was leaving everything unfinished. Someone else would have to solve all the problems, and to Gerber that didn't seem right. But he had no choice. He just hoped that

Henderson didn't think that he was running out on him, leaving him holding the bag.

Neither man voiced the idea. Gerber did his best to tell Henderson everything he could that would help the new commander rebuild the camp and control the strikers. He made sure that Henderson understood that the acting ARVN camp commander, Lieutenant Minh, was the best Vietnamese officer that any of them had ever met. Gerber suggested that they try to get Minh named permanent commander. Gerber decided it was about the only thing he could really do for Henderson.

The next morning, Gerber shook hands with Henderson, wished him luck, and then boarded the helicopter that would take him and his battered team to Saigon.

The short flight didn't give them much time to sleep. Gerber had tried to get the pilot to orbit the camp, but after circling it twice, the pilot wanted to head home. Over the back of his seat he shouted, "You give Charlie time to set up by flying orbits and he'll shoot your ass out of the sky."

Gerber nodded and held a thumb up. He could understand the logic of that, and he had seen everything that he needed to see. Much more than he wanted. Besides, there wasn't a lot that he could do about it now anyway.

Touching down at Ton Son Nhut, it occurred to Gerber that he was spending a lot of time in Saigon. It also occurred to him that every time he came to Saigon, something happened at the camp. He hoped for Henderson's sake that tonight would be the exception.

Unlike the last time, there was no jeep to meet him. There was no transport for the team. They stood there for a few moments, wondering what to do, until Gerber had them pick up their gear and head toward the edge of the field.

It took them twenty minutes to walk the distance to Bates's B-team headquarters. Gerber told them to drop their stuff in the outer office and then go over to the club. He would talk to Bates and then come to find them.

Ten minutes later he was back in the outer office, trying to place a call to Nha Trang. Bates had said that he had secured an extra seat on the plane, if Gerber thought that he could find someone to use it. Gerber decided not to look a gift horse in the mouth and told Karen Morrow, a flight nurse in the air force at Nha Trang, that the plane would leave the next day, about two in the afternoon. Her orders, the necessary papers, were all ready, if she could get the approval of her commander.

"Make him understand, Karen, that we're not trying to take over his command. We're just offering an opportunity if you can get him to let you take advantage of it."

On the other end of the line, Karen hesitated. "It's been pretty slow here for the last week. We've had the chance to catch up on a lot of backlogged paperwork. Most of the wards are empty. Still, I don't know."

"You can ask. That won't hurt. And you'll only be gone a week."

"No, it won't hurt to ask." She was silent for a moment, almost as if she was afraid to say what was on her mind. Finally she said, "How are you?"

"Tired. Extremely tired. But I'll get over that."

"Good." She stopped and then continued. "Listen. It might take me a while to get an answer. Where will you be?"

"I don't know. You can leave a message here and I'll probably get it."

"Tell you what, Mack. If you don't hear from me, you can expect me there tomorrow. If I can't make it, I'll leave word around for you."

"Please get here."

She hesitated again, wanting to ask about the attack but afraid to say anything. They were both avoiding the subject because they knew that they couldn't discuss anything on the phone. The connection was bad at best, and it didn't allow for the intimacy that would be needed. So, rather than ask about the attack, she said, a little too happily, "I'll see you tomorrow."

"Right," said Gerber. He hung up.

The plane, a TWA Boeing 707, sat on the ramp, waiting for its passengers. Gerber paced the waiting room, looking for Karen. She had not called and she had not arrived. When boarding instructions were issued, Gerber waited at the end of the line, hoping that Karen had been delayed but would still arrive. In front of him were the other members of his team, all dressed in civilian clothes. They looked like a bunch of soldiers who had been told to wear civilian clothes and who had gone out and bought the first things they found. There were mismatched shirts and pants and shoes. Not one of them looked comfortable in the new clothes.

Gerber was the last to enter the plane, but he got a window seat, courtesy of Sergeant Fetterman. In fact, there were three seats together. Fetterman had the aisle, Gerber the window, with the empty seat between them reserved for Karen.

At the moment that Gerber had finally decided that she hadn't been able to make it, one of the doors of the terminal swung open, and Karen, carrying an olive-drab suitcase and wearing a purple dress, rushed through.

They closed the door of the airplane as she entered and hustled her down to the waiting seat. A stewardess took the suitcase to put in a storage area in the rear of the plane and told her to buckle up because they would take off immediately.

When the stewardess disappeared, Karen, breathing hard as if she had just run a long way—like through most of the terminal and across the ramp—put a hand on Gerber's and said, "I didn't think I would make it."

"Neither did I," said Gerber, smiling. He pointed at the man next to her. "This is Tony Fetterman. He's my team sergeant."

Fetterman smiled at her and said, "Glad to meet you."

Karen, forgetting herself, said, "Yes, I remember. He was the one who came to find you that last night."

Gerber shot her a glance, and she realized that Gerber had never told Fetterman that she had been in his room when Fetterman arrived to announce the impending attack on Camp A-555.

There wasn't a word from Fetterman. He just smiled as if he understood everything totally. Which he did.

After the plane took off, Gerber and Karen talked about a lot of things. But the flight was long, and Gerber soon fell asleep. In fact, most of his team had gone to sleep long before he did. They hadn't gotten a lot of sleep in the last week, and the party they had started at the NCO club the night before had continued until nearly six.

They landed in Darwin, Australia, where a lone man got on to spray the plane, explaining that they were trying to keep various types of "communist germs and insects" out of Australia. Then the plane's captain explained that they would be on the ground for a while because the airport at Sidney was closed until seven A.M. for noise abatement procedures.

When they landed in Sidney, they were escorted into a large room where they were briefed on some of the things they had to know about Australia. They were warned that they shouldn't rent a car because the right-handed driving on the left side of the road quickly became confusing, and although there were no laws or regulations prohibiting them from driving, taxis were plentiful and very cheap.

They were given a list of hotels and told to select one. A bus would take them there and they would be allowed to register. They were told what time the bus would pick them up for the return flight. They were told where to report if they missed the bus and what time to be there so they wouldn't miss the flight back. Finally they were told to have a good time but to remember that they were in a foreign country and not do anything to embarrass the United States or make the Australians regret allowing them in.

Together, Karen and Gerber selected a hotel in the King's Cross area, unaware that it was the last stop on the bus line. Then, with the little luggage they had, they boarded the bus and left.

Bowing to convention, they registered separately, getting two rooms, with Gerber wondering if they would really fool anyone or if anyone would care. They went upstairs and separated long enough to check on the rooms. Gerber was disappointed that there was no bathtub. He was tired of cold showers and had longed to sit in a deep, hot bath. But the tiny bathroom only contained a shower. At least the water would be hot.

He turned on the TV and spun the dial, just to see what was on. Then he looked out the window toward the building thunderclouds that suggested a late summer shower. At a quiet tap at his door, he turned.

In moments, Karen was in his arms and they were kissing deeply. Gerber rubbed his hands over her back, almost as if to assure himself that she was real.

Finally she pulled away slightly, breathing heavily and staring into his eyes. "I was afraid for you."

For a moment, Gerber didn't understand what she meant. Then he remembered their last meeting, when he'd been whisked away to the camp already under attack. He said, "There was nothing to worry about." He knew it sounded lame. Unbelievable.

Karen stepped away and looked at the tiny room that held two twin beds, a low dresser with a TV at one end, and a small refrigerator at the other. There was only one chair near the windows that overlooked the street. She moved toward the chair and then thought better of it. She sat on the bed and leaned back on her hands. She knew that it was too soon, that they should have a few more moments together, yet she had to know. She said, "What was it like?"

Gerber waved a hand, trying to wipe the question out of the air. "Just like you would think it would be."

That didn't satisfy her. She had spent a sleepless night in Saigon, waiting to hear about him after Fetterman had come to take him back to the camp. She knew the camp was going to be attacked and she was afraid that Gerber would be killed. She had waited, hearing rumors about the assault, about the camp being lost, almost lost, being held, being wiped out. The rumors had flown around Saigon like snowflakes in a blizzard because it was the biggest battle fought to date in the war, and although no one knew anything about it, they all wanted to sound as if they did. All her questions were answered, but the answers were wrong. No one understood the importance of the questions.

Now, with Gerber in the room with her, she could think of nothing else. She wanted to know what it had been like because she didn't want to spend another night wondering. She had to know, and until she did, things would not be right between them. She couldn't let it go until later. It was like a barrier that had to be climbed first.

Gerber looked at her and, in a flash of insight, understood exactly. He stared at her, almost as if seeing her for the first time. Her soft brown hair hung to her shoulders, and her blue eyes, even now, sparkled with a light that made them seem to be full of mischief. She was tall and slim. Her ankles were small and her calves were curved almost to perfection. But it was her quick mind, her high intelligence, and self-reliance that had originally attracted him.

Finally, he pulled the chair around so that he could look at her and said, "I guess you could say it was rough. We nearly lost the camp. It was very close."

Quietly, she asked, "Will you tell me about it? Please. I need to know."

"Yes. If you really want to hear. It's not very pretty."

"I know what it's like," she said. "I *do* work in a hospital and I see the results."

Gerber nodded. "Of course. It's just . . ." He stopped, thought, and said, "It's just that I haven't really thought about it at all. Haven't had the chance with everything that has happened since."

"I'm sorry, Mack. But I have to know. I really do."

"It's okay. It just might take me a few minutes to get organized."

She reached out and touched his arm. "You don't have to go into detail. Just a little bit so that I can understand."

"After I left you," Gerber began, "Fetterman had a helicopter waiting to take us back to the camp." And with those few words, he was suddenly out of the room and in the bouncing aircraft, heading toward the camp that was nearly, but still not quite completed.

He told how his executive officer, Lieutenant Jonathan Bromhead, advised him on the radio that it was the real thing. The enemy buildup was nearly complete and they were beginning to take heavy mortar and rocket fire.

The pilot dropped down, hoping that a low approach would go undetected, but the VC saw them and opened fire. The helicopter crashed. No one was killed. Gerber and Fetterman organized the people so that they could sneak into the camp. They hadn't traveled very far when they found a VC mortar crew. Using knives, Gerber and a couple of the strikers that Fetterman had brought as a "bodyguard" moved in. When the VC were dead, Gerber had his people pick up the mortar tube and enemy weapons, and they headed toward the camp.

Before they could get there, they ran into about forty VC, who opened fire as soon as they saw the Americans. "We were pinned down," said Gerber. "Couldn't move any direction, so I tried to call for a mortar attack. Bromhead wanted to send out a patrol but I said no. Lieutenant Minh, the ARVN XO, however, organized a platoon and came out to get us. Together we chased the VC away long enough so that we could get to the wire.

"Once we were inside, I ran to the fire control tower. From there I could see that we were surrounded by nearly a regiment of VC. They launched the attack almost at once. Bromhead left the tower to direct the fight on the west wall where it looked like the main thrust was going to come."

And at first it did. Gerber explained how the assault there was broken, just as the attack began in the south. There, Lieutenant Minh directed the fighting, which quickly became hand-to-hand. Two of the Americans, Sergeant Clarke and Kepler, ran down to help. By this time, there were VC inside the camp, and Clarke and Kepler ran into them. Kepler killed one of them by hitting him over the head with an ammo can.

The defense on the south wall began to collapse, but Gerber could do nothing about it. He had abandoned the fire control tower, after it was hit by rocket and mortar fire, to command the east wall. They could see one, maybe two battalions forming up out there to attack.

Now Gerber lost his train of thought. He wasn't sure what had happened on the other walls because he had been so busy himself. He knew that Fetterman, with his flamethrower, had managed to prevent the west wall from falling once.

Gerber stood and walked to the window. The rain had finally started and was streaking grimy glass. Without turning around, he continued. "They began a surging charge across the paddies, screaming and yelling and blowing their bugles. We opened fire but it did little to check the advance. Sergeant Smith had electrified one rice paddy. That, combined with the shooting from our side, stopped them. The charge broke."

Karen, staring at Gerber's back, felt relief surge through her. They had stopped the assault. And from the way he said it, she thought it was about over.

"Then, looking out, I saw another battalion. Not the remains of one, but a whole new one. They began the attack again. This time we had no tricks left. No claymore mines. The heavy weapons were down and we were running out of ammo. They overran the wall.

"There was nothing I could do. I ordered everyone to fall back to a secondary line that I thought we could hold. I was trying to get to Bocker in the commo bunker so that I could find out why the air support hadn't arrived."

Now Karen stood up and moved to Gerber. She leaned her head on his shoulder and said, "I'm sorry. I had to know."

Gerber reached up and patted her hand. "It's all right. We got out. As I reached the commo bunker, I heard the air force pilots and told them where we needed to have the air strike. We combined that with the mortars, right on the wall, barely breaking the assault. We rallied the ARVNs and Tais and managed to retake the wall. There wasn't much of it left, but it did give us some protection. That last seemed to have broken their back because they began to withdraw.

"That was it. The VC abandoned the attack and headed for the border. We didn't try to follow or get a blocking force in because we didn't have the manpower left to do it. We were lucky to get out."

Gerber felt that the end of the story left something to be desired. He couldn't explain his whole role to her. How it felt when the bayonet penetrated the enemy's flesh or how the hand-to-hand fighting had really been. How could he tell her that he had shoved his pistol into the stomach of a man and pulled the trigger? Those were the things that no one ever really talked about.

And Karen knew that there was more to tell. There were hundreds of details that she could ask for, but she didn't want to hear them. She knew what she had to know. She turned Gerber around so that he was facing her, and then she kissed him, pulling him toward the bed.

But now there was something else between them. Gerber was visibly upset by having to recall everything about that night. He had managed to push it away. He didn't regret telling Karen, only that now there seemed to be some kind of apparition between them.

Together, they sat on the bed and leaned back. But Gerber hesitated. He rolled to his back and stared at the ceiling.

Karen felt the change in him and started to move away, but Gerber caught her and held her. He didn't want to do anything else right then, except hold her. Surprisingly, in minutes, he was asleep.

When she was sure that Gerber had gone to sleep, she slipped away from him, amazed that he didn't react. She had seen soldiers in the hospital come wide-awake at the slightest sound, including the quiet squeak of the rubber-soled shoes the nurses wore. One of the soldiers had told her that it sounded just like the noises made by the rubber-soled sandals worn by the VC.

But Gerber didn't react. Apparently he subconsciously knew that he was in a safe environment. He slept on.

Karen carefully took off her dress and hung it up. Then she went into the bathroom and took a long, hot shower. Toweling herself, she wished that she had brought her powder. Then she dressed only in her stockings, garter, and panties.

Back in the bedroom, she lay down beside Gerber, who stirred slightly but didn't wake up. He shifted once and then settled down.

An hour later, Gerber opened his eyes. He saw Karen and smiled at her. She kissed him lightly and he said, "Hey. Wait a minute. Let me, at least, brush my teeth."

In the bathroom, he decided to try the shower quickly. He stripped, turned on the water, and stepped in, adjusting it until it was nearly too hot to stand. Then, rather than washing himself, he just let the water splash over him, forgetting everything.

Karen entered the bathroom without a sound, picked a washcloth off the rack near the sink, and climbed naked into the shower. She began to wash Gerber's back. All he did was look and smile.

She washed all of him, starting with his back and working her way down slowly, sensuously. Then she made him turn around and started washing his feet, his legs, and then slowly, lightly rubbing his groin, noticing an immediate reaction. She smiled up at him and said, "Thanks. That makes it easier to wash."

When she finished, she kissed him and said, "Are we through?"

Gerber looked at her in mock horror. "Are you crazy? You're filthy. I'll have to wash you." He took the cloth and began to soap it. Carefully he washed her shoulders and then worked down to her breasts, which he rubbed slowly, finally using both hands.

She stepped close to him, pushing herself against

him and trying to kiss him. Gerber resisted, using the washcloth to massage her stomach.

In the cramped space of the shower it was hard to move, but Gerber managed to step back. Again he soaped the washcloth so that he could wash her legs, taking his time on her thighs.

That done, she said, "Let's get out of here before my skin wrinkles up."

Gerber shut off the water and reached out for a towel. When Karen did the same, he said, "No, I'll take care of this." He then began to dry her slowly, first her legs, then her back, and finally her chest. Then he dropped the towel and began kissing her at her shoulders, working his way down, while she shuddered in anticipation and desire.

Later, lying in bed and watching the shadows creep across the ceiling, Gerber managed to turn off his mind. He wasn't thinking about anything. He was aware that Karen was next to him and could feel the heat of her body. Out of the corner of his eye, he could see her. But he was drifting in and out of sleep, not really aware of much else.

The knock at the door startled him. His whole body tensed, causing him to jump nearly off the bed. He fell back, breathing hard and shaking from the adrenaline that had pumped into him.

Karen looked at him, at first concerned, and then asked, "You want me to get that?"

Gerber got up. "No. I'll do it."

When there was another knock, he called, "Just a second. I'll be there."

Pulling on his pants, Gerber hopped to the door.

He just buckled his belt and opened up the door. There was a man who looked like he worked in the hotel.

"Are you Captain Gerber?"

"Yes."

"I have a telegram for you."

Gerber reached out and took it. He rummaged in one of his pockets, found an Australian dollar, and gave it to the man.

"Thanks," said the man.

Gerber closed the door and ripped open the envelope. From across the room Karen said, "What is it?"

He didn't answer. He just read the first few lines and said, "I don't believe it. The son of a bitch demands we take R and R and now this."

Karen stood and said, again, "What is it?"

"We're being recalled. We've got to get back to Saigon."

"All of us?"

Gerber looked up and said, almost to himself, "No. Just the team and me. You can stay."

"That's not what I meant," she said.

"Says use first possible flight. Report immediately to Bates."

"But . . ."

Gerber slowly crumpled the paper into a tight ball and tossed it at the window. "Damn it all."

Karen said, "You don't have to leave until tomorrow do you?"

"I don't suppose," said Gerber, looking at his watch, "that I'll have much luck finding everyone else and getting the flight arrangements made before tomorrow."

"Then come over here and let's discuss it." She

dropped the towel she had been holding in front of her naked body. "You can find Sergeant Fetterman and have him call the others, can't you? In a little while."

"Yeah," said Gerber. "I can call Fetterman after a little while."

Folding herself into his arms, she said, "Do you know what it's about?"

"No. But since they're recalling us, I imagine that it is going to be bad news."

Standing there, in the hotel room in Australia, he had no idea how bad the news could be.

CHAPTER 2 _____

U.S. Army Special Forces Captain Mack Gerber wondered what the trouble was. He knew it had to be trouble of some kind. That was the only possible explanation for the telegram from Colonel Bates ordering his return to Saigon ASAP. Gerber hoped the A-team replacing them out at the camp hadn't been hit by the VC. When he walked through the door into Bates's outer office, the unexpected appearance of Lieutenant Bao, commander of the Tai strike company at Camp A-555, hit him like a slap in the face.

Bao assured Gerber, however, that everything was running smoothly at the camp. Lieutenant Minh had been made ARVN camp commander, although it was too soon yet to know if the appointment would be permanent. In the aftermath of the fierce battle less than a week ago, the camp was being temporarily reinforced by two companies of ARVN rangers until troop strength could be brought back up to normal. Colonel Bates was also known to be pushing for

33

funds and approval to form a second company of Tai strikers for A-555, to be permanently based there. General Crinshaw, strangely, had not protested the additional manpower. Apparently he had been pleased with the media coverage back in the United States of the victory over the main force Viet Cong AWF regiment.

Gerber's team sergeant, Fetterman, arrived a few minutes later, with Sergeants Smith, McMillan, Bocker, and Tyme in tow. Except for Fetterman, who was chipper as a chipmunk, albeit considerably less chatty, all were bleary-eyed and clearly suffering from the morning-after blues, but all looked suitably military in their pressed jungle fatigues and green berets.

As soon as all were present, the administrative sergeant behind the typewriter picked up the telephone and buzzed the colonel's office, then nodded at them to go on in.

Bates greeted each man warmly, then closed the door to the outer office and turned serious.

"Mack. Gentlemen. I'm sorry to have to break up your fun just when you were getting started. You guys needed the break, and it's a shitty deal to snatch it away from you like this, but it can't be helped. Something's come up that demands immediate action, and you people are the only ones available. I won't bullshit you by telling you that nobody else could do this job. Special Forces is full of people who could do it. The simple truth is none of them are available. If I could have picked anybody else for this, I would have, because I know what you men have just been through. The sad fact is you guys are it, because you're all I've got."

"Colonel," said Gerber, "are you telling us we've been picked for a suicide mission, or to baby-sit some visiting VIP?"

Bates smiled. "Neither, I hope. Right now, all I can tell you is that it is a matter of vital importance to our national security, and that it involves going north."

"May I ask how far north, sir?" said Fetterman.

Bates smiled again. "Right now, let's just say somewhere north of Hue and south of Red China. Interested?"

Gerber glanced at his men. All were leaning forward expectantly. Fetterman had a grin on his face so wide it made Gerber's teeth hurt.

"My men seem to be of the opinion that there's nothing like carrying the fight to the enemy, sir," said Gerber. "I would like to know exactly what we're getting ourselves into, however. How much more can you tell us?"

"Only that it involves going up north. But not to fight, if possible. It involves bringing something back. It's important. There's a time element involved, and I'm getting a lot of pressure from higher up to do something fast. Either you guys give it a go, or I tell higher-up that it can't be done."

"Colonel, you're really asking us to buy a pig in a poke."

"I know that, Captain. I wouldn't be asking if I didn't think it was important. There are people very high up, that's capital V, capital H, capital UP, who have spoken to me via secure channel in the last forty-eight hours. On the surface of things, I'd agree with them that it is important, but just how important I didn't fully realize until I started getting all the phone calls. It was the status of the people making the calls that convinced me, if you understand what I'm saying."

"That still doesn't tell us much."

"I'm sorry Gerber, but right now, that's the way it's got to be. Damn it, man. I'm trying to give you guys an out, here. You *can* say no to this one. But you've got to do it now. Once you know the details, it's too late."

"Okay, Colonel. You don't have to do a James Bond number on us. If it's that important, you got yourself a volunteer. I won't presume to speak for the rest of my men, however, since you've made it clear that it is on a voluntary basis."

Fetterman, Smith, and Bocker nodded rapidly. Tyme stood still for a moment, then nodded thoughtfully.

"I suppose these crazies are going to need someone to look after them," said McMillan. He was the senior medical specialist on Gerber's A Detachment. "Count me in too, sir."

Bates looked at Bao. "Well, Lieutenant? It's got to be unanimous."

The wiry tribesman shook his head. "I sorry, Colonel, but I not understand why we do this thing. You say we go north, but not fight. Instead of fight, you say we bring something back. I am soldier. Trained to fight. Trained to kill Cong. I pretty good soldier. I kill pretty good bunch of Cong. What you say sound like maybe steal something. Man who steal is thief. I soldier, not thief. I fight Cong, okay, but I not steal. Bao no thief."

"Of course not, Lieutenant," said Bates. "But I am not asking you to steal something. The Cong have stolen something from us, two somethings. And we want them back. It is not stealing to take back something someone has stolen from you, is it?''

"No sir, I guess not. These things you want us to steal back from Cong that he steal from us, they help us win war?''

"They might. I can't guarantee that.''

Bates could see that he was going to have to say something more to convince Bao, but didn't know what.

Finally, Bao said, "If I do this, Colonel, it maybe not help win the war, but I help your country?''

"Yes. It would do that.''

"Colonel, I not know you very well, but I think you are an okay guy. I know all these men well. They all A-Number-One. All Green Berets I meet at camp A-555 A-Number-One. They risk their lives to help me free my country of Cong and bring peace here. Especially Lieutenant Johnny, who get much hurt in fighting at camp. I much like Lieutenant Johnny. He like a brother to me. I, how you say, I love Lieutenant Johnny. I do anything to help him. What you talk about still sound like stealing, but I tell you this. Lieutenant Johnny, him almost get killed helping me to fight for my country. If this thing help Lieutenant Johnny's country, then I do it, even if it is stealing. But I want Lieutenant Johnny to tell me it is okay. I not steal for you. I not steal for Captain Mack and these men, although I much like them. But I will steal these things whose names you cannot tell us if Lieutenant Johnny tell me it must be done.''

Bates stared thunderstruck at Gerber, who could only shrug his shoulders. Both men knew that Bao had developed a very close relationship with Gerber's executive officer, Lieutenant Jonathan Bromhead, during the construction and subsequent defense of Special Forces Camp A-555. Neither man had realized how much that relationship meant to the Tai tribesman.

"Okay. You two go have a talk with Bromhead," Bates said at last to Gerber. "But be very careful what you say. You never know who might be listening. The rest of you go look busy somewhere until after lunch. Don't discuss this with anybody. Not even among yourselves. Captain Gerber, I'll expect you and Lieutenant Bao back in my office at 1300 hours, with the lieutenant's answer. I want the rest of you back here at that time also. That's it. Dismissed."

As they walked away from Bates's office, Gerber shook his head in amazement at the convolutions the mission was already beginning to take on.

I've got to convince Bromhead to convince Bao to go into North Vietnam to steal back something we've lost up there, and I don't even know if it's people or pretzels, he thought. Hell. It would have been simpler baby-sitting some VIP. Wheels!

"Captain Gerber! Bao! Gee, it sure is great to see you guys. You've no idea how boring it gets around here, sir," said Bromhead. Then he added, "Say, I thought you and the rest of the team drew an R and R, sir. What are you still doing here? Miss the plane?"

"Leave got canceled, Johnny," said Gerber, unconsciously lowering his voice as he glanced around the hospital ward. The nearest patient was three beds away.

Bromhead noticed the captain's glance. "Slow season around here," he said nonchalantly. "Or so the nurses tell me. Not much going on out in the war, I guess. Still, you got to be field grade to rate a semiprivate room. Only a general can get one to himself."

Gerber nodded absently. "How are you feeling?"

"Fine, sir. Still got a little ringing in my ears, but the docs tell me that'll go away in a week or so. They got most of the shrapnel out too. Said the rest of it isn't where it'll matter much. Just too inconvenient to dig it all out, I guess."

Bromhead lowered his own voice. "I gather, sir, that this isn't entirely a social call. Something big is up, right?"

Gerber moved closer to the bed and dropped his voice all the way down to a whisper. "We were already swilling down pints of Foster's Lager in Sydney when we got a hurry-up telegram from Colonel Bates, telling us to repack our duffels and get back here ASAP. The air force, or somebody, has lost something up north, and they need us to go get it back for them."

"Up north, huh? As in capital 'North'?"

Gerber nodded slightly.

"Right, sir. If you'll just help me find my pants so I can walk out of here without attracting too much undue attention, we'll go get it for them. We might have to have Doc McMillan saw this damned cast off though before I can—"

"Whoa! Wait a minute! You just hold it right there, soldier. You are not going anywhere until the doctors say you can."

"Don't be silly, sir. Of course I am. I said I felt fine. Besides, you said they needed us to get it back for them."

"That's not exactly why we're here, Johnny. I'm taking half the team. The uninjured half. At least the fit for duty half. Small scrapes, scratches, and cuts don't count. I'm also taking Bao, here, if he'll go. The problem is, he doesn't want to. That's why I brought him over here. I was hoping you might be able to talk him into going."

Bromhead stared at the Tai tribesman with some surprise. He knew the man was no coward. "What's the matter, Bao? Why don't you want to go?"

"I not afraid go, Lieutenant Johnny. I not like leave my men, but Sergeant Hung, he good soldier. He take good care of them, keep them from getting zapped while killing too many VC for Sergeant Krung. I put Hung in command, make Krung his XO, they work okay together. Also Minh run camp now. Him good soldier, good fighter. Him good man. Too bad him born Vietnamese. We make him, how you say, we make him hon-oh-rari Tai."

"We say 'honorary' Tai." Bromhead smiled. "I'm glad to hear that. I like Lieutenant Minh too. He's a fine soldier. But why don't you want to go with Captain Gerber?"

"Your Colonel Bates, him say northern Cong have something he want us to go get. That sound like stealing. I tell him I not steal, not thief. I tell him I soldier trained to kill Cong. But him say we not to kill northern Cong. Just go take this thing. Him say we must not shoot at northern Cong unless they shoot at us first. Then we must run away and still not shoot. We only get to shoot northern Cong if can't run away. Coward run away, not Tai soldier. I not thief, not coward. Not want to steal something, then run away like coward. In this, there is no honor.''

Bromhead felt a twinge of sympathy as well as a certain pride in the naiveté of this simple, honest man. He spent the next fifteen minutes trying, not altogether successfully, to explain to Bao why what was being asked of him was neither cowardly nor dishonorable. In the end, it all came down to one thing.

"You tell Bao this, Lieutenant Johnny," said the Tai. "You believe it is okay to do this? You would do this yourself and feel no shame?"

"If Colonel Bates and Captain Gerber say it is important, their word is good enough for me. They are honorable men, Bao, and would never ask me to do anything dishonorable, or do anything dishonorable themselves. If they would do it themselves, or ask me to, I would do it and feel no shame. Especially if it's as important as they say it is."

"But you do not even know what it is we go to bring back!" protested Bao.

"No. I do not know. And I do not need to know until the time comes to actually bring it back. It might be a person or a thing. That would make no difference. I would do it because I know these men, and because they tell me it is important, and ask me to help. I would help them as I would my own brother.''

Bao nodded gravely. "Then it is so. As you would help a man you would be honored to call your brother,

I would help same. The man who would be your brother, would be mine.''

He turned to Gerber. "We go tell Colonel Bates everybody goes.''

After meeting with Gerber and the others in his office at one o'clock and being assured that Lieutenant Bao was now willing to accompany the mission, Colonel Bates took the men across the sprawling military base to an empty briefing room in the Operations Center. When a guard had been posted at the outer door and both it and the inner door had been locked, Bates introduced them to the man who had been waiting for them to arrive.

"Gentlemen, this is Mr. Tucker Wilson. He's from Langley. Mr. Wilson will give you a mission synopsis. You'll receive a detailed area study and briefing once you go into isolation for mission prep at Nha Trang.''

The mention of Nha Trang brought Karen immediately to Gerber's mind. He pushed the thought of her quickly aside. He couldn't tell her about this, and wasn't sure he'd want her to know. He probably wouldn't even be able to see her at Nha Trang. Talk about lousy luck!

As Wilson stood up on the little stage, took a pointer in hand, and pulled the roll-up map down from the ceiling, Gerber couldn't help thinking he'd have known the man was CIA instantly, even if Bates hadn't said he was from the Central Intelligence Agency's headquarters in Langley, Virginia. Well, Bates hadn't said that, exactly. He'd just said the man was from Langley. He'd expected them to be smart enough to be able to figure the rest of it out

for themselves. Gerber wondered momentarily how
he was going to explain a concept like the CIA to
Lieutenant Bao. That might prove tricky. The rest of
it didn't matter. The guy had "super spook" written
all over him.

Wilson was dressed in a white shirt and khaki
pants and had on a tan bush jacket with a large bulge
under his left armpit. He had a head of thick, silver
hair and a tan complexion. He might have been
anywhere from forty years old to sixty. The smooth-
shaven face betrayed no signs of age.

Wilson took a pair of glasses out of his pocket,
held them in front of his face while he consulted
some papers, then folded the papers and put them in
a pocket of the bush jacket. He returned the glasses
to a case in an inner pocket, took the pointer out
from under his arm, and addressed the group.

"Gentlemen, today's briefing is classified top secret,
and is not to be discussed outside of this room.

"Late Thursday afternoon, last, a U-2 high altitude reconnaissance aircraft piloted by Air Force Major M. F. Jessup, flew a mission over a certain area
of interest in western China. Following that, Major
Jessup also investigated a certain area of interest over
southeastern China. Major Jessup's final destination,
due to various considerations of the mission, was
here in Saigon.

"Major Jessup had completed the active part of his
mission and was en route to Ton Son Nhut when he
encountered unexpectedly heavy anti-aircraft missile
fire approximately here, near the village of Son Tay."

Wilson touched the map briefly with the pointer
stick.

"Major Jessup was able to evade part of the missiles but suffered damage to his aircraft, and was forced to bail out somewhere in this area here, just north of the North Vietnamese coastal village of Mo Ron."

Again the pointer touched the map.

"Intelligence from certain sources leads us to believe that he was captured upon landing and subsequently taken to another small village nearby, known as Nhu Ky. We believe the North Vietnamese Army has a small military garrison there."

He touched the pointer to the map a third time, then tucked it under his arm like a swagger stick.

"Our mission is to go in and get Major Jessup out before he can be persuaded to talk by the North Vietnamese, or be transferred to another locale where more sophisticated means of interrogation may be available. We'll be doing a HALO drop from a sterile C-130 at 25,000 feet. Upon assurance that we have landed without detection, we will proceed to the village of Nhu Ky and reconnoiter the North Vietnamese encampment in an attempt to ascertain whether or not Major Jessup is in fact being held prisoner there. If we succeed in determining the major's physical presence, we will then attempt a rescue. Upon effecting the rescue or determining that Major Jessup is no longer present at the target location, we will then make our way overland to the coast, north of Mo Ron, where we will be exfiltrated by SWIFT boats and taken to a rendezvous with naval destroyers in international waters.

"As Colonel Bates has indicated, a detailed area

study and mission profile will be provided, along with suitable equipment when we reach Nha Trang.

"Are there any questions at this point?"

The team members waited for their commander to speak first.

"What makes you believe Jessup is still in Nhu Ky?" asked Gerber.

"As I mentioned, we have information from certain sources indicating he was taken to the garrison there after his capture. The exact nature of those sources is classified on a need-to-know basis, in order to prevent their compromise. I'm afraid you gentlemen don't have the necessary need-to-know. All I can tell you is that he was taken to Nhu Ky and was not seen to leave."

"How current is your information on that?"

"The information is current as of 7:45 this morning."

"He could have been moved since then, or he could still be moved before we can get there."

"Quite true. Time is of the essence. However, it does take a certain amount of time to mount an operation of this sort. We'll be going up to Nha Trang later this afternoon for preparation. The actual jump will be made just before dusk tomorrow night."

Sully Smith gave a low whistle. "That is mounting a clandestine op on short notice. Especially in totally unfamiliar terrain."

"Granted. We'll have maps and aerial photos to work from, but we'll have to depend a good deal on basic fieldcraft. It can't be helped. The only way this mission has a chance of success is by utilizing the element of surprise to the maximum. If we appear to be too interested in the area, they'll know something is up and move Jessup before we can get to him.''

"You keep saying 'we,' " said Gerber. "Am I to take it that you will be going along on the operation?''

"That is correct. The necessary clearances and orders have already been issued. You gentlemen have, so to speak, been put on temporary loan to me.''

"Then perhaps we'd better clarify the command structure before we get out into the field." Gerber didn't like the sound of it, having a civilian in charge. Baby-sitting VIPs was beginning to look better to him all the time.

"Rest easy on that score, Captain," Wilson told him. "You will be in operational command and make all decisions of a tactical nature. However, I am authorized to, and shall, make any decisions of a policy nature that should become necessary."

Gerber didn't like the sound of that much better, but let it pass.

"What kind of equipment will we be using for the drop?" asked Fetterman.

"The parachutes will be a West German commercial sport model, similar to the one you used for HALO training, Sergeant, but lighter, more comfortable, and slightly more maneuverable."

"Fine. Also, just to satisfy my idle curiosity, I thought the U-2 was supposed to fly above the effective range of the surface to air missiles. How did the NVA manage to shoot this guy down?"

"Good question, Sergeant. It's one of the things we want to ask Major Jessup when we get him out."

"I've been wondering about the composition of our little team," said Bocker. "Wouldn't it make more sense to send in a couple of companies of rangers, or the Marines, to get this guy out?''

"It would if we were planning a prisoner rescue operation on a typical POW camp. However, we're talking here about getting one man out. That makes secrecy and surprise of the utmost importance. As I said, if they suspect we're up to something, they may move him. They might also simply kill him. Besides, political considerations make a large-scale raid an unviable option at this point in time.

"You men have been selected because you've worked well together before, under hostile conditions, and because you were available close at hand, on short notice. Further, each of you is a specialist in an area crucial to the outcome of this mission. You, Sergeant Bocker, are a communications expert. Sergeant Tyme is a small arms specialist. Sergeant Smith is a demolitions genius, I'm told. Sergeant McMillan, as a senior combat medical specialist, may well be called upon to ply his craft on Major Jessup, since the NVA has a policy of vigorous interrogation. Captain Gerber is a logical choice for a tactical commander, and Master Sergeant Fetterman, his NCO counterpart, is an administrative specialist. Also, he's had extensive experience in line crossing operations and deep penetration. Besides, he has certain physical attributes that may prove useful and is proficient with a variety of highly unusual weapons, which we may find desirable to employ. Lieutenant Bao is a member of the Nung subgroup of ethnic Tai peoples and may prove helpful should the need arise to make contact with the Nung tribesman who coinhabit the area, along with the North Vietnamese. Also, he does not suffer from the same sort of security problems that we've experienced in the past with some of our ARVN friends.''

Bocker knew what the man meant. South Vietnamese security had more holes in it than a sieve. ARVN was infiltrated by VC informants and sympathizers at virtually all levels. The Tai tribesman and other Montagnard groups employed as mercenaries by Special Forces suffered from no such infiltration problems, since in most instances they disliked and frequently despised the ethnic Vietnamese, whether communist or not, whom they regarded as having stolen their country from them many centuries ago. Some, like Bao, had learned to work with the noncommunist Vietnamese as well as the Americans, since they were fighting the VC whom the tribesman hated most of all, because of their frequently brutal treatment of tribesmen, but even Bao did not care for most of the lowlanders he'd met.

''I have a final question,'' said Gerber. ''It would seem to me that the film in Jessup's reconnaissance camera would be of somewhat more use than Jessup himself. Undoubtedly, the quality of the optics enabled the camera to see much more than Jessup possibly could have. Why the man and not the machine?''

''That's a rather cold-blooded question, Captain,'' Wilson admonished.

''Not at all. It's a practical one. Any man here would do whatever he could to rescue a downed pilot before he could fall into enemy hands. But why risk eight men to try to save one who's already in enemy hands, and may even be dead by now for all we know?''

"I see the point. Well, I've already mentioned the need to debrief Jessup on how he was shot down when he should have been well beyond the range of SAM-2s. If the communists have succeeded in significantly enhancing the range, that is, the maximum altitude of their SAMs, then it is vital that we know about it. Also, it is standard procedure for a U-2 pilot forced to abandon his aircraft to destroy the camera and its film, along with certain other equipment of a sensitive nature. The aircraft is provided with a number of short, time-delay self-destruction charges for that purpose, and we assume Jessup would have activated these charges before bailing out. This prevents the enemy from gaining knowledge of the nature and operating characteristics of these sensitive systems, and from knowing exactly what it is that we were interested in photographing and how good the pictures were. If Jessup threw the switches as he was supposed to have done, then there is no machine, as you put it, to recover. Unfortunately, we don't know that Jessup was able to activate the destruct charges. Doing so can be a tricky business while you're trying to get out of a stricken aircraft. If Jessup wasn't able to activate the charges, then a number of our most sophisticated systems, particularly electronic countermeasures, may well be compromised. Such a compromise could well put our entire air force, as well as naval and Marine aviation, in serious jeopardy. I need hardly tell you what implications that could have for our national security. SAC's nuclear deterrence capability could be brought into serious question, and our ability to project tactical or strategic airpower in a conventional conflict would lack credibility. We don't know that Jessup was able to destroy his camera and ECM equipment. That's something we've got to know. And the only way to know is to ask him.

"Are there any more questions?"

"I have question, please."

It was Bao.

"Yes, Lieutenant. What is it?"

"Explain, please, what is 'hay-low.' "

There was a stunned silence. Gerber finally broke it. "My God! I never thought of that. It just never occurred to me."

"Of course," said Bates slowly. "I don't know why I didn't think of it. I suppose it was just because all of us are HALO-qualified, so I just naturally assumed . . ."

Realization was slowly beginning to dawn on Wilson's face.

"Colonel Bates, Captain Gerber, surely you don't mean to say that . . ."

"That's right," said Gerber. "Lieutenant Bao doesn't know what a HALO drop is. He's never done one. In fact, he's never made a parachute jump of any kind!"

CHAPTER 3 _____

From the moment they arrived, they were in almost complete isolation. At the airfield, they were met by a man dressed in jungle fatigues but who wore no insignia or patches. He pointed to the gear and then to a deuce-and-a-half, and said, "You can put your gear in there." Without another word, he turned and climbed into the cab.

Gerber looked at his team and shrugged. He picked up his duffel bag, tossed it into the back, and jumped up. He stood and waited while the others followed suit. When everyone was on board, including Wilson, Gerber knocked on the rear window of the truck. They started off with a lurch that nearly toppled Gerber into Fetterman's lap.

From the other side of the truck, Tyme asked, "What happens now, Captain?"

"I wish I knew," Gerber answered. "You guys know as much about this as I do. Maybe Wilson knows."

"I'm sorry, Captain, but at this point I don't know any more than you do," Wilson said.

51

"There you have it," said Gerber. "Nobody knows anything."

Fetterman spoke up. "I think, all things considered, I'd rather be in Australia. There was a young lady there who seemed to be interested in exploring some of the more intimate regions of the human body."

"What about Mrs. Fetterman and the kids?" asked Smith.

"Mrs. Fetterman and the kids wouldn't deny me a little R-and-R pleasure. Besides, there wasn't time to get into trouble, thanks to the captain."

Now Gerber spoke up. "And you know very well that I had nothing to do with that."

"Yes sir. Nothing at all."

The truck stopped and the driver got out. He appeared at the rear and said, "You'll be staying in the hootch over there."

He then stood aside while Gerber and the team unloaded their gear. When that was completed, he got back into the cab and drove away.

"Let's get this stuff stored," said Gerber, shouldering his pack and starting toward the hootch.

Inside, he dropped everything on the dirty plywood floor, looked up at the ceiling fan that wasn't turning, and then saw Bates standing in the corner. Gerber said, "Thought you'd be in Saigon."

"I should be, but someone has to guide you through the last few hours here."

"And how many of those do we have?"

"Depends on the weather."

The rest of the team was pushing its way in. Fetterman carefully set his pack on a table and said,

"I thought this was one of those right-now-let's-run-a-mission missions."

"There is a little slack built in and we want to use that to obtain the optimum weather," Bates said.

Once everyone was into the main room of the hootch, Bates said, "There were a couple of things that we didn't discuss in the general briefing. And I've got a package of aerial photographs and maps of the target area. The maps, unfortunately, are fairly old, but with the photos, we should be able to piece together an accurate picture.

"And I've brought the weapons and parachutes you'll be using. There is a set of camouflage clothes for each of you. Everything is from Europe for obvious reasons."

Fetterman moved to the center of the room, looked at Bates, and said, "Where are the chutes? I'd like to take a look at them."

Bates hitchhiked a thumb over his shoulder. "In there. They've been packed by a couple of master riggers attached to the Special Forces here. The chutes are like the HALO model of the Type-10 steerable you've used, so you all should be familiar with them."

"I don't suppose you'd mind if I take a look at them," said Fetterman.

"Go right ahead. You'll find the weapons in there too." Now Bates smiled. "Got most of them from your old camp. There's an AK for each of you, along with a couple of silenced weapons, an RPD, and an RPG-7."

"How much warning will we get?" asked Gerber.

"An hour at least. Weather decision will have to

be made by 1900 hours so that you can be on the ground before daylight. We were going to put you in tomorrow at dusk, but conditions are deteriorating so fast over the drop zone that it looks like you'll be going in tonight. Any other questions?''

Several of the team members shook their heads. Sergeant Tyme asked, ''Will we have a chance to zero the weapons?''

''Afraid not. There's nothing around here that would allow that.''

''Come on, Colonel,'' Tyme protested. ''There has to be a range.''

''Oh there is. But we can't have you guys test-firing a bunch of AK-47s. There is no secure location around here.''

''Great,'' mumbled Tyme. ''Night drop into enemy territory with unfamiliar weapons and maps that are out-of-date.''

''Anything else?'' asked Bates. When no one said anything, he said, ''Please don't leave here. An evening meal will be supplied about 1700. There are cards, magazines, and a radio. I'll see you with a decision by 1900.''

After Bates left, Tyme walked into the room where Fetterman was examining the parachutes. Tyme picked up one of the AK-47s, pulled back the bolt, and looked into the chamber. He let the bolt slide home and sighted along the barrel. Next he picked up a thirty-round magazine, inserted it, and jacked a round into the chamber. He removed the magazine and worked the bolt again, ejecting the shell.

"Well, the weapons seem to have been well cared for. Works smoothly. Wish we could fire them."

Fetterman looked at him. "It's all right, Boom-Boom. I'm sure that the weapons were carefully selected, and should be sufficiently accurate. Besides, we're not going to be doing any long-range sniping."

"Sure. Says the man who is checking the work of a couple of master riggers, just to be safe."

Gerber entered the room, walked to the parachutes and looked, moved toward the weapons, and then over to the other supplies, including the camouflaged fatigues that were of West German design. He reached down for one of the combat knives, took it out of the sheath, and saw that it was nearly razor sharp. To Fetterman he said, "Looks like they're giving us the best they have."

"Yes sir. Sure hope they know what they're doing."

"I know what you mean."

At 1700 hours, a truck pulled up outside, and Bates waved from the cab. The back opened, and three men, all wearing Special Forces patches and booney hats, got out. They lifted down several large, hot food containers, which they carried in and opened.

Bates, who had followed, said, "We've got steaks, chicken, baked potatoes, corn, and green beans. The best we could do."

Sully Smith, who had been fairly quiet, said, "Why do I feel like the condemned man who gets the hearty last meal?"

"That's what we need," said Fetterman. "A little lighthearted banter."

"Or in Smith's case," said Tyme, "light-headed."

Interrupting, Bates said, "We've even prepared a special meal for your Lieutenant Bao."

"Oh-oh," said Smith. "The plot thickens."

"Now, come on," said Bates. "We're only trying to make things a little more pleasant. Besides, this might be the last hot meal you get for a while."

"I wish you wouldn't say last," said Smith.

At 1900 hours Bates returned, driving a jeep. As he opened the barbed-wire gate that separated the hootch from the rest of the compound, he shook his head. Gerber immediately assumed that it meant the mission was off. Once inside, Bates confirmed it.

"It's a no-go for tonight. I think we have to go tomorrow, even if we don't have the weather."

"I don't suppose we'll get to use any of the facilities here," said Smith. "Like the NCO club."

"Or the range," Tyme added pointedly.

"I'm afraid not," said Bates. He looked at Gerber as if he knew that Gerber was thinking of the abruptly canceled R and R and that Karen had returned to Nha Trang. "I'll see what I can do about securing the range for a couple of hours tomorrow afternoon."

When Bates left, Gerber, Fetterman, Wilson, and Bao studied the charts that they had been given. A potential DZ had been noted on the charts, and several routes to the site of the camp had been drawn. But no one had been there, so the charts could be inaccurate and the photos distorted. All they could do was try to memorize as many landmarks as they could and then play it by ear.

*   *   *

They spent the next day working with the equipment, learning the idiosyncrasies of the weapons, and familiarizing themselves with everything else. They also tried to break up the piles of equipment into equal parts so that they would be better able to carry it. In the beginning, loads would be heavy, but as the mission continued, as they used the food supplies and ammo, the loads would become lighter.

By late afternoon, Gerber was sure that there was nothing else they could do. Given the circumstances, they had done it all.

In the early evening, Bates showed up with a light dinner. As the food was spread out on the table in the center of the room, he said, "I really think we're going tonight. After you eat, you should start to get ready. Official word will come in about an hour and a half."

The C-130, with the national insignia painted out, was parked at the end of the runway, close to the hootch but away from the rest of the base. When Bates gave them the word, all the Americans dressed in the camouflage fatigues, donned the equipment, and left the hootch. Bao followed, dressed in black pajamas and carrying a conical hat along with his jump helmet.

Before they left, Gerber burned all the maps and photos, except for a couple that he carried for reference. Except for the Russian weapons, they were the only things he had that didn't come from West Germany. The maps were French.

The ramp at the back of the aircraft was down, waiting for them. The engines were running as they boarded. The load master beckoned them in and yelled over the noise of the props to take a seat on either side. He told them to store their equipment in the center of the plane, near the back. Once they were all on board, he raised the ramp, motioned them to buckle their seat belts, and then sat down himself.

The plane lurched forward, the noise increasing until it was nearly impossible to talk. Moments later, they raced down the runway and took off. As they climbed to altitude, the engine noise decreased slightly.

The flight engineer sat down next to Gerber and yelled in his ear, "We're going to have to land in Da Nang to refuel. Some foul-up. Although it's normally not procedure, we're going to refuel with you guys on board. If the plane blows up, I guess the AC will be in a world of shit." He smiled and moved off.

Gerber watched the sky darken for a few minutes, and then the pilot turned on the red lights for the back of the plane. They didn't use white because that would ruin their night vision, although Bocker was unconcernedly smoking a large cigar. When it was nearly black out, Gerber leaned over and said to Fetterman, "How's Bao going to be?"

"I don't know, sir. This is going to be a wonderful jump. I'll bet even money that he breaks an arm or leg. I mean, a night jump with virtually no training, he's practically guaranteed to break something. I just hope it isn't his neck."

Across the aisle, Tyme was tearing down his weapon to clean it again, although it was in perfect working order. Smith was reading a *Playboy* that had seen better days. McMillan was pawing through his medical bag again, wondering if there was something in the first-aid kits on the plane that he could steal. And the mysterious Tucker Wilson was staring placidly into space.

Gerber looked at his map once more, trying to memorize everything he could about the DZ. But the red light washed out some of the landmarks and writing. Fetterman was sitting with his eyes closed, probably asleep already. Bao was trying hard not to look scared, but he was not only going for a plane ride—something he had done only once before, and that on the way to Nha Trang—he was going to have to jump out of it. Bocker was still puffing away, watching the smoke drift around the interior of the plane.

Just as the flight engineer had said, they landed at Da Nang to refuel. Gerber and his team did not get out, and as far as anyone at Da Nang knew, there were no passengers on the plane. In less than thirty minutes, they were airborne again. This time the pilot turned out all the lights in the back of the aircraft.

Outside, Gerber saw the navigation lights of a small plane. He pointed it out to the flight engineer, who said, "Fighter escort. There are four of them out there."

"Hell of a note," said Fetterman without opening his eyes.

"What's a hell of a note?" asked Gerber.

"Whoever heard of a super secret mission with a fighter escort?"

An hour later, the plane made a slow descent until it was less than three hundred feet above the jungle. They turned due north, from a position well inside of Laos. They flew on for half an hour, turned to the east, and crossed into North Vietnam. The flight engineer yelled, "About fifteen minutes."

They made a rapid ascent, reaching 25,000 feet. The load masters and flight engineer put on oxygen masks with long hoses so that they could breathe when the airplane was depressurized for the jump. Each man on Gerber's team had a small oxygen bottle that would allow him to breathe for about ten minutes after they had jumped from the aircraft. At the altitude they were operating at, if they hadn't had the bottles, they would have remained conscious for less than half a minute.

The aircraft made a sudden turn to the right and then leveled out. Through one of the tiny windows, Gerber saw the lights of one fighter flash and then vanish. He didn't know if the pilot had turned them out or not. It didn't seem to be a good idea to be flying over North Vietnam with all those lights on.

The flight engineer held up a hand and flashed a sign at Gerber, who unbuckled his seat belt and then reached over to tap Bocker on the shoulder. Bocker would be acting jump master because Fetterman would be jumping while holding on to Bao's harness. They would go in the middle of the stick.

Bocker took his position near the right troop door and yelled, "Stand up. Check equipment."

With that done, Bocker looked at the flight engineer, who held up five fingers. Bocker yelled over the noise, "Let's go to oxygen."

As soon as that happened, they all felt their ears pop and the air in the aircraft became cold as the pilot depressurized the plane. When the small light came on near the troop door, the flight engineer stepped forward and unlocked it, pulling it in and pushing it up, out of the way. That done, he moved back, so that Bocker could take his place at the side of the group of men.

A red light came on and the flight engineer looked at Bocker, who had already seen it. Tyme moved forward to stand in the door, since he would be the first out.

The timing of the jump was critical. The DZ would be almost impossible for them to see. The pilots of the C-130, conferring with the pilots of the fighters, had pinpointed the DZ as best they could based on dead reckoning, pilotage, and even celestial navigation. One of the planes had broken away from the formation for a low-level pass. Everything indicated that they were right over the target area.

When the light went to green, Bocker tried to slap Tyme on the shoulder, but he hit only empty air. Tyme had already jumped. McMillan was right behind him, followed by Tucker, and then Fetterman and Bao together. Bao was clinging to Fetterman so hard that his knuckles and hands were white. Bao had his eyes closed tightly.

Sully Smith was next, then Gerber, and finally Bocker. As soon as they were all out, the flight engineer closed the door, but the aircraft stayed on its flight route for several miles in case they were being tracked by radar. It would then turn and descend, popping up to altitude a couple of times in other places to confuse the enemy as to the exact location of the drop zone.

Gerber looked back in time to see Bocker jump. Then he looked down but could see nothing except inky blackness and a few shapings of gray. He hoped that the pilots and navigators had been accurate. It was now too late to worry about that. But if they came down in triple canopy jungle, they would all probably break arms and legs and be captured inside a week. If the rats didn't eat them first. Or if they didn't break their backs. Or their necks.

Gerber stretched himself out in a full arch position to stabilize his descent. He searched for the others, but they were hidden by the darkness, appearing only fleetingly, as shadows. He would have to trust in luck to put them all in the same location.

In the darkness, it was difficult to see even the highly luminous dial of the barometric altimeter fixed to the top of his reserve container. At 1500-feet altitude, Gerber brought both hands in to his harness, the right automatically finding the D-ring, gripping it tightly. Pushing his hands back out, he pulled the ripcord of the main parachute, felt the pilot chute pop from the main container upon his back, dragging out the canopy bundle, pulling the folded suspension lines free from their rubber-band retainers, pulling the main canopy free at last from the deployment bag.

Gerber heard the rustling of nylon fabric as the canopy slipped free from the D-bag and filled with air, heard the muffled opening crack, and felt the deceptive sensation of a sudden upward tug as the canopy braked hard into the air, checking his descent. And then there was silence. Sudden. Absolute.

Immediately glancing overhead, Gerber checked the condition of his parachute, found that he had a good deployment with a full 360-degree canopy with no sign of snarled suspension lines or blown panels. The only holes in the fabric were the steering and drive slots and the vent hole in the center of the canopy designed to prevent oscillation. Gerber breathed a sigh of relief. Now all he had to worry about was landing without breaking anything.

When the altimeter read two hundred feet, Gerber used the steering toggles to turn the canopy so that it would face what he hoped was into the wind. He checked the area below him a final time for obstructions, but it was too dark to see anything. All he could do was hope the air force taxi had let them out over the DZ and that no one had drifted too far off course. It was a fairly large DZ, but for a night jump from high altitude, it wasn't all that big. Gerber prepared for a tree landing by putting his feet together, knees slightly flexed, tucking in his chin, and placing his hands in opposite armpits, palms out, bringing his arms up in front of his face to protect his eyes.

Seconds later, he felt his feet strike the ground. As the canopy tugged him over backward, he immediately executed a reverse PLF. As he struggled to get to his feet, the canopy billowed out and tried to drag him across the DZ. Lacking the quick release buckle normally used on the harness for low-altitude static line jumps with military parachutes, Gerber quickly snapped down the right safety cover that protected

the capewell securing the canopy riser to his harness,
stuck his thumb through the ring, and pulled hard.
The capewell released and, unanchored on one side,
the canopy sheared away, spilling out its air and
collapsing.

Acting quickly, he got to his feet and gathered in
the canopy and lines, then checked his compass and
made his way rapidly for the northwest edge of the
pitch-black DZ.

He dropped the parachute there, found some cover,
and waited until he could see another human moving
toward him. Using the challenge code they had agreed
on, he said, *"Dos."*

The man whispered, *"Cinco."*

Gerber didn't think using Spanish numbers for the
challenge would fool the North Vietnamese. It was
just one more way of trying to hide their nationality.
Like using the West German equipment.

The man dropped his parachute on Gerber's and
crouched beside him. McMillan said, "I'm the first?"

But as he said it, Gerber saw two more men. He
said *"Tres."*

"Cuatro."

Bocker and Wilson had arrived. Gerber didn't say
a word. He just pointed to the right side of the DZ.
Bocker took off toward it so that he could cover their
flank. McMillan didn't have to be told what to do.
He slipped off to the left, finding a position just
inside the trees. As he was leaving, Smith showed
up. Tyme crawled up a second later and added his
parachute to the pile.

Twenty minutes later, neither Fetterman nor Bao
had arrived, and Gerber was beginning to worry. It

wasn't like Fetterman to be late or to miss a rendezvous. Gerber whistled softly, calling back Bocker and McMillan. Smith was quietly digging a hole under a bush near a large tree to bury the parachutes and equipment containers so that the DZ would be clean. In fact, Smith and Bocker were going to wait until first light so they could check the DZ for anything that might have been missed in the dark. They would catch up with the others once that was done.

To the group, Gerber said quietly, "Anyone see either Fetterman or Bao? No? Okay, I suppose we'd better begin looking for them."

"Captain," said Wilson, "we don't have time to go looking for any missing men. They'll just have to take their chances."

"I'm afraid that if we don't find them, Mr. Wilson," countered Gerber, "we're going to head straight back to South Vietnam. We won't be able to complete the mission if they're missing because we'll have to assume that we've been compromised."

For a moment, Wilson was silent. Then, almost to himself, he said, "They're not going to like that."

Gerber didn't have to say anything more. The men spread out along the edges of the DZ and began a quiet search. Gerber walked straight to the center, stopped, and tried to look around. All he could see was the dark ground, the darker trees, and the not quite so dark gray of the sky, peppered with stars. He crouched on one knee, surveying his surroundings, but found no clue of Fetterman and Bao.

He moved the rest of the way, crossed the clearing, and entered the trees, walking carefully so that he made no noise. He wasn't overly worried about boobytraps because he didn't think that the North Vietnamese would boobytrap their own backyard.

He hadn't gone very far when he heard a soft call that sounded like an owl. That was the last thing that Gerber expected to hear in a North Vietnamese jungle, and he moved toward the sound.

He found Tyme, who said, "Nothing."

"Let's head back. We've got to do something quickly. We can't hang around here much longer."

As they reached the rally point, Gerber heard something in the trees. He said, *"Cinco."*

"Dos," came the unmistakable voice of Fetterman.

Gerber moved toward them, and when he saw both Fetterman and Bao lying on the ground, he said, "Where in the hell have you been?"

"Bao broke his leg."

"Oh, Christ. How bad is it?"

"Only a simple fracture, but he's not going to be able to walk easily."

Gerber moved forward and looked down. "How are you feeling?" he asked Bao.

"I told Lieutenant Johnny that it not a good idea for me to jump out of airplane, especially before engines quit and propellers stop."

Gerber helped Fetterman lift Bao and together they carried him to the rally point. They set him down and Gerber said, "I suppose we'll have to make a litter."

"You mean carry him?" asked Tucker.

"Of course. We can't leave him and we need him to make contact with the villagers. We have no choice."

"But that will slow us down."

"Not that much, especially at night. We can't go

crashing through here like elephants. We have to move slowly so that we don't make noise and we don't leave sign.''

''Then the mission is on?''

''What did you think?'' asked Gerber. ''Of course the mission is on. We move out in fifteen minutes.''

CHAPTER 4 _____

When Tyme and Fetterman finished making a stretcher, McMillan gave Bao a shot to help him sleep. Wilson stood to one side, complaining under his breath about the waste of time. Gerber had tried to explain that they couldn't leave any wounded behind. Bocker and Smith were scouring the DZ, trying to hide anything that might give them away.

Fetterman stepped up to Gerber and said, "Anytime. There's not a whole lot more we can do."

"You get a compass reading?"

"No sir."

Gerber took his compass out and watched as the luminous needle swung until it was pointing to the north. Gerber turned the compass so that the N was under the needle. He would have set it on the map to orient himself but couldn't because there wasn't enough light, and he wasn't going to light one. Besides, he had studied the map enough so that he was fairly sure where he wanted to go.

68

Gerber said to Tyme, "Why don't you take the point? Head off in that direction, about 346 degrees for about an hour and thirty minutes. Then we'll find a place to hole up for the day."

Digging through one of his pockets, Tyme found his own compass, checked it against Gerber's, and said, "Okay, sir. Who's going to carry the stretcher?"

"We'll rotate the duty. I'll take one end and Mc-Millan can take the other to start."

"I guess I'll take off, then."

"We'll follow in a couple of minutes. Remember, don't use your weapon unless it's absolutely necessary."

As Tyme disappeared into the trees, Gerber moved back to Bocker and Smith. "You guys get out of here as soon as possible. I would suggest waiting for daylight just inside the trees; that way you'll have a chance to escape if someone stumbles onto the DZ."

"We'll follow just as soon as we can."

"Good. Use a heading of 346 degrees. We're not going to go too far tonight. Just enough to get us well clear of the DZ. See you in the morning."

"Yes sir," said Bocker. "Good luck."

"Captain," said Sully Smith, "I've got a question. Should we leave any boobytraps here?"

"No, Sully. We want to be like a light breeze. Leave nothing behind that will suggest we were ever here. Toward the end of the mission we might want to scatter a couple of things, but not now."

From out of the darkness, Fetterman said, "We'd better shake a leg or Tyme will get away from us."

Without another word, they moved off, spreading out. Staying close enough together so that they could just see one another, they moved slowly, trying to set each foot down quietly, avoiding snapping twigs and rustling leaves. Even carrying the stretcher, Gerber and McMillan had good luck at it. Wilson, on the other hand, trained in something other than jungle warfare, couldn't keep quiet. And he didn't like the slow pace. He wanted to move rapidly, but speed through the jungle only made noise. Gerber finally told him to take one end of the stretcher, hoping that would slow him down.

Back at the DZ, Bocker and Smith finished scouring the area and then moved to the trees, near where they had begun the hole to bury the parachutes. Smith jumped down into it and began digging again. In a few minutes he had it deep enough, and Bocker tossed the parachutes to him. Once they were in the hole, he covered them with a layer of dirt but didn't completely finish burying them. He wanted to wait until they made sure the DZ was clean.

Bocker helped him shovel some of the dirt back into the hole. Then both of them moved away to a large bush that gave them a good view of both the hole and the DZ. They crawled under, facing in opposite directions, their feet touching so that each knew that the other was still there. No one could sneak up behind them because one of them would see.

Dawn wasn't far off. Although they couldn't see the east sky begin to lighten, they knew that it was. Around them the jungle erupted in sound as the monkeys came awake. They all seemed to howl and screech, as if they wanted everything in the jungle to awaken.

Smith turned around and nearly yelled at Bocker to make himself heard over the ruckus. "What the hell?"

"It's nothing. They do it every morning. Heard the same thing once in the Philippines."

Ten minutes after it began, the noise tapered off and finally faded. Around them was a lot of movement, most of it made by the monkeys that had been howling, but some of it made by large animals on the ground. Although Bocker and Smith heard them, they didn't see them.

Bocker finally turned around and said, "You stay here. I think it's light enough to see. I'll check the DZ one last time."

He moved out from under the bush, crouched near a tree, and carefully checked the area. He saw nothing out of the ordinary and headed for the center of the DZ. There he found a parachute packing slip and one can of C-rations that had somehow gotten out of a pack. He also found several deep footprints that he did his best to obscure. He picked up the stuff and moved back to the hole. He tossed the paper in, saving the C-rations which could still be used.

Just as he picked up the E-tool to finish burying the parachutes and waste, he heard a bark of laughter. Without waiting, he dived for cover. Seconds later, a group of men, all carrying weapons, strolled out onto the DZ.

Bocker slipped under the bush, moving back until his feet were in contact with Smith's. He eased his AK-47 to his shoulder and took off the safety. At the moment, he didn't plan to use it, but he wanted it to be ready.

The enemy, only six of them, had walked to the

center of the DZ and stopped. One of them ran off,
as if to gather wood, while two others scraped at the
grass, clearing an area about five feet in diameter.
The last three stood around watching for a moment,
then one of them crouched down, opened a pack, and
began extracting food. Each of them kept his weapon
close.

Smith had turned around so that he could whisper
in Bocker's ear. "You think they're looking for us?"

"Nah. They're too casual. If they had some idea
that we were in the area, I think they would be a little
more careful. And there would be more of them."

"Surely they're not patrolling."

"Could be. We're not that deep into North Vietnam.
Or it could be some kind of training exercise."

"And they pick today to wander around here?"

"Coincidences happen. They'll be gone soon and
we can finish up and get out of here. The others will
wait."

The North Vietnamese had started a fire and stacked
their weapons near them. One of them was cooking,
using a pot that looked far too big to carry around on
patrol. They were talking and laughing among
themselves, giving the impression that they were just
out on a lark and not a military mission. It reminded
Bocker of the National Guard on a weekend drill.

For an hour, Bocker and Smith lay under the bush,
watching the enemy as they ate their breakfast. The
sun was now high overhead and they could see wisps
of steam rising from the grass as the early morning
dew burned off. It wasn't hot yet, but all the signs
were there. It would be soon.

Bocker had finally convinced himself that there

was nothing to worry about. As he had said to Smith, this wasn't a search party. It was just bad luck that they had stumbled onto the DZ before he could finish burying the equipment and disappear into the jungle.

One of the enemy separated himself from the group and began walking toward them. He hadn't brought his rifle but had a long knife.

Bocker pushed himself farther under the bush, looking around to make sure that there were no tracks or signs exposing his hiding place. The enemy soldier, however, didn't seem to be interested in looking for signs.

The man entered the trees, found a small bush, and dropped his pants as he squatted. He stayed there for a few minutes while the others called to him, pointing and laughing. When he finished, he stood up and used a palm branch to scatter some dirt over the area.

Bocker thought they were going to get away clean. Then he saw the pile of dirt and the hole that he and Smith had dug. Part of one chute was exposed, and he hadn't had time to throw any dirt on the debris he had found. It stood out, almost like a neon sign. But none of the North Vietnamese had shown any inclination to search the DZ.

But the man with the palm branch was moving toward the hole now. He tossed the branch away and called to his friends. Still he hadn't seen anything. Then he turned, looked right at the hole, seemed to ignore it, but began to walk toward it.

Bocker tapped Smith on the shoulder as he drew his knife. He eased forward, trying to make no noise. He slipped out from under the bush, crawling around a tree so that he could move up behind the enemy soldier who was standing on the edge of the hole, looking down into it as if it held something fascinating.

The enemy soldier dropped into the hole and picked up the packing slip, turning it over in his hand as if he had never seen anything so interesting. Bocker, using the tree to shield himself from the center of the DZ, reached the edge of the hole. The man's back was to him. Bocker waited until the man stood up, but before he could shout, Bocker grabbed him, pulling him back. With one hand over his mouth and nose, Bocker jerked upward and slashed at the throat, nearly severing the head. The man spasmed, kicked his feet, and then died quickly and quietly.

Bocker dragged the body into the trees and hid it under a bush for the moment. Then, rather than trying to hide himself under the bush with Smith, he moved behind it where he could watch the other five. Smith now worked his way out from under it so that he would be able to move around easily.

In the DZ the other soldiers were still eating and laughing. Once or twice they called out to the man who was now dead. At first the voices were taunting, but then they became concerned. Finally one of them broke off from the group and headed toward the bushes where the first man had disappeared.

He strolled up, calling to his missing comrade. He was kidding around, as if he believed that his friend was hiding as a joke. He walked around a tree, right into Bocker, who killed him as quickly as he had the first man.

But now, those in the DZ were becoming worried. Even in the north, you just didn't disappear into the woods without some kind of explanation. The other four picked up their weapons and spread out.

Bocker slid back, away from the body of the dead man. Smith, without a word or signal, moved to the left, toward a large tree. He hoped that it would offer him some protection. And he eased the safety of his AK-47 off, figuring that he would have to shoot.

As the enemy entered the trees, between Bocker and Smith, one of them disappeared from sight. He had found the body of one of the men and stooped to look at it. Not a survival trait. Bocker hit him in the back of the head with his rifle butt with enough force to snap his neck. He died before he knew that he had been hit.

Something seemed to change in the air. The last three enemy soldiers seemed to realize that something was wrong. As one, they backed out of the trees, their weapons covering them. There was a whispered conversation, a hesitation, as they watched. One of them called softly out in Vietnamese, the voice quiet and concerned.

Then, without warning, they opened fire. Bocker dropped to the ground, as if wounded. Smith saw him fall and thought he was hit, but Bocker held a thumb up. The bullets whistled through the trees over their heads.

Slowly, the firing tapered off as all three emptied their weapons. One of them slapped a new magazine in and fired a final burst at an unfortunate monkey who had screeched a protest at them.

Bocker slid his weapon forward and pointed it at the enemy soldiers who were now walking backward toward the campfire. He nodded at Smith, who understood immediately and did the same. At a second nod, both opened fire on full automatic.

All three enemy went down, but only one had been hit. They had been waiting for something to happen, and at the first sound they dropped. For a second they were quiet, and then they started shooting.

Bocker rolled left, to the other side of the tree, and fired another burst. Smith stayed in one place, now firing single shots as he saw movement. Neither side was doing any more damage.

The firefight became a trading of shots. Bocker suddenly realized why the Vietnamese weren't moving. They were in their own territory and figured that someone would eventually be along to help. Bocker wanted to jump up and rush them, but knew that would not work. The Vietnamese had found the perfect place. Open ground all around them with a little cover to offer protection. Bocker and Smith were the ones in trouble. They could break off the engagement and slip away, but they couldn't afford to leave the Vietnamese alive.

Bocker got to one knee, hoping he could see something that would help. He was about to move when a burst of firing, followed by two grenade explosions, shattered the center of the DZ. Then, from the trees, to his right he heard Fetterman say, "Can't you clowns do anything right?"

Bocker didn't answer. He leaped to his feet and sprinted toward the center of the DZ. He found the bodies of the Vietnamese lying near their fire. All three were dead. He picked up their weapons and called, "It's clear."

Fetterman stepped into the DZ. He said, "Let's get out of here. We've wasted enough time."

"What about the bodies?"

"Drag them to the hole where the parachutes are and we'll bury them too. But we've got to hurry." Fetterman pointed to Tyme who had come in from the other side of the DZ. "Boom-Boom, sweep the area to make sure that we've policed up everything. Get the weapons and equipment, but don't worry too much about the fire. If the Vietnamese find it, they'll know that their people were here. Probably figure that they moved off on their own. Throw some dirt on it and get rid of the pot."

"You don't really think that anyone will be fooled?"

"Doesn't matter. As long as everything remains hidden for two, three days, we'll be okay. It's not like we're going to live here."

It took only thirty minutes to dig the hole deep enough to hide the bodies. They threw in everything the enemy carried, except for weapons and ammunition and a couple of wallets that seemed to contain some interesting identity papers. Fetterman rolled them into a handkerchief, reminding himself that he would have to destroy them if it looked as if they would be captured. To be found in enemy territory, in unmarked uniforms, carrying enemy weapons and the wallets of enemy dead, would be to sign their own death warrants.

They covered the bodies and the parachutes and everything else with a thin layer of dirt. Then, from about a hundred yards off, Tyme and Fetterman pulled up a couple of small bushes to transplant over the hole. Neither man thought the bushes would live long, and they would soon point to the hole rather than hide it, but they would be good for a couple of days, and that was all that was needed.

An hour after Fetterman and Tyme had arrived, they were ready to move out. Tyme again took the point, able to move faster because he now knew where he was going. Besides, it was daylight. That made travel a little easier.

Gerber had heard the firing in the distance but had rejected the idea of sending anyone else. Besides, there weren't others to send. If they hadn't returned, he would have scrubbed the mission: no chance of succeeding with four men missing.

But soon Tyme appeared, and then the others. They briefed Gerber about the fight. Gerber said, "Then I guess we had better move out of here. We're too close to the DZ, especially now."

Wilson butted in again. "Is it a good idea to move in the daylight?"

"Probably not," responded Gerber. "But we don't have much choice. You heard the firefight, and the odds are that someone else did too. We're not far enough away. We'll be able to travel a little faster in the daylight."

"And you'll leave the gook now?"

Gerber gave Wilson a withering stare. "That gook is named Lieutenant Bao. He is a loyal, intelligent ally. And he is valuable, perhaps even key, to this mission. We will carry him." Gerber shook his head. "Given the choice, Wilson, I would prefer leaving you behind. I don't know what importance you have to this. We can get along without you. Now quit making stupid suggestions.''

McMillan diffused the tension, saying, ''We're ready to go. Bao should be okay. The break isn't causing him any real problem.''

''Right.'' Gerber moved over to Fetterman. ''You want to take the point?''

''No problem. How far you want to move?''

''Four or five miles. Then find somewhere to hole up for a couple of hours. After dark, we'll start again.''

''You think we've been compromised?''

Gerber rubbed his chin and looked at his team sergeant. ''I don't know. That damned fight could really hurt us. If there was no one around to hear, we might be okay. The real key is that we don't have to have everything hidden forever. Just a couple of days is all. That's the critical thing.''

Before Fetterman moved out, Gerber said to Bocker, ''You want to bring up the rear? Make a quick sweep through here to make sure that we didn't leave anything behind.''

Bocker grinned. ''Stuck with the cleanup detail again.''

''Don't take too long. Just a quick sweep. Same thing applies here. If it can't be easily seen, then it will probably stay hidden long enough.''

They started off, staying clear of the trails and pathways, not because they feared boobytraps but because they might run into someone else using them. Then, to maintain secrecy, they would have to eliminate anyone they saw. Anyone. And if too many people disappeared in too short a period, suspicion would be aroused. So they took the hard route, moving quietly and carefully, but quickly. Gerber didn't like even the minimal amount of noise they were making with their rapid pace, but figured that it didn't matter too much. Anyone else would likely be making more noise, and Gerber hoped that he would hear them before they heard him. That was the way it had to be, or the mission would be over permanently.

Around them, they could see, periodically, small animals, lizards, and an occasional snake. Gerber didn't like the snakes because he was afraid that they were all poisonous. On entry into Vietnam he had been told that there were one hundred varieties of snakes there and ninety-nine of them were poisonous. The other one would swallow you whole. He knew that it wasn't quite true, but it was close enough for government work. He kept his eyes open for them.

The ground around them was cleaner than he expected. In triple canopy jungle, by the time you reached the ground, there was little sunlight for green plants. The traveling wasn't easy, there were creepers and wait-a-minute vines, but it wasn't as difficult as it could have been.

After fifty minutes, Fetterman found a place to rest. He sat down. Seconds later the others arrived. They scattered, Tyme and Smith looking for places where they could cover the others. Bao was asleep on his stretcher. Bocker came up a few minutes after that. He had found nothing that would give them away.

The ten-minute rest was not nearly enough, but Gerber knew they had to push on. There was the possibility that the DZ and the dead men would be found. Any moment, there could be an alert. Gerber didn't know how good the communication system in the area was. It might be days before the word was passed, or it might be minutes.

Again they moved out, following the compass as closely as they could. Now Smith was at the point. Fetterman and Bocker formed a rear guard. McMillan and Wilson were carrying Bao. Gerber enjoyed seeing Wilson working like that since his only purpose on the mission seemed to be to complain.

Near midafternoon they found the perfect campsite. There was a source of water close by and good cover. They spread out, found hiding places, and ate a quick, cold meal. Since the mission was to be relatively short, they had opted for the extra weight of some West German combat meals—heavier, but more tasty than freeze-dried food, and not requiring heat or extra water. Rather than carrying the whole meal, they had taken out the best parts—the peaches, or the applesauce—leaving behind the nearly worthless canned bread, soda crackers, and ham and lima beans.

Gerber ate his peaches, scraped a hole near the roots of a bush, and buried his can. Then he took one swallow of water, checked his weapon, and closed his eyes. At the moment, Wilson was on guard duty. Since Gerber didn't trust him to do the job right, Tyme was also on duty. Later, Gerber would take a stand at it, and then Fetterman. At ten o'clock, they would move out, hoping to reach the prison camp by dawn.

In the dark, the going was slower. The ground was uneven and they had to move carefully, checking ahead of themselves with sticks to make sure they didn't walk into a ravine or fall into a hole. They used one path for a while because they were falling behind schedule. It was a risk, but it wasn't like the south where there would be VC or American patrols out, where there would be ambushes and boobytraps, and where all their movement would be observed by farmers and villagers who were VC sympathizers. Here, they hadn't seen anyone, other than the soldiers who had stumbled onto the DZ.

And even though Gerber told himself that it was the right move, each step on the path was frightening because there was so much to go wrong. But they had to make up the time. They had to hurry because they didn't know how long the Vietnamese would keep Jessup in the camp, or how long the guard detachment would be kept at its small number, or if a large, important contingent from Hanoi would arrive to interrogate the prisoner or transfer him. That would mean a lot of enemy activity, and they couldn't afford that.

At one of the rest stops, Bao said that he thought he could walk, as long as he had some kind of crutch. Tyme slipped into the trees, found a sapling that was about the right length and had the right shape. Bao tried it and found that he could actually move quite well with it. McMillan wasn't sure how wise it was to let him try to walk, but it would eliminate the hassle of the stretcher. Besides, there wasn't that much farther to go.

After the short rest, they took off, moving faster

now. Again, they followed a path, but this seemed to be more of a game trail than a path. That it was a game trail changed everything, since they didn't know what kind of game used it or if predators hunted along it. All they needed was for some large cat to pounce on them.

But they ran into nothing. It was less than thirty minutes before dawn when the point man dropped to the ground. Gerber crawled up for a look.

Wilson came up behind him and demanded, "Why have we stopped?"

Gerber pointed and said, "We're here."

CHAPTER 5 _____

The camp was different from those they had encountered in Cambodia and South Vietnam. That was to be expected. This was Charlie's home ground. This was North Vietnam.

As Gerber studied the enemy camp from his carefully concealed position beneath the edge of a thicket on a high ridge overlooking the camp from the west, he could make out clearly the four-meter-high barbed-wire fence set on wooden telephone poles that completely surrounded the compound. Through the excellent Steiner binoculars he'd been provided with at Nha Trang, he could almost see the bored expression on the face of the single guard in the lone watchtower located near the center of the camp. The guard at the double gate on the south side of the camp did not appear much more alert, and the sentry shuffling slowly around and around the outside of the wire might have been walking in his sleep. Apparently the guards were very unconcerned about any possible security problems, despite the assumed presence of their American prisoner.

Gerber had seen the same type of lackadaisical attitude before when he had taken half his team and Bao's company of Tai strikers across the border to hit VC sanctuaries in Cambodia. Charlie felt safe there, because he knew the rule that forbade Americans from crossing that imaginary line that divided Cambodia from South Vietnam, a line the communists themselves crossed daily. Charlie had been wrong, and Charlie had died.

But this camp was different. The solid fence, the wooden-frame barracks, the low painted concrete administration building with the corrugated metal roof, the scattered lights set on high poles, all combined to give the camp a more permanent, more military look. It was the look of a slightly seedy, slightly rundown, small military garrison, of course, but that was perfectly normal. That was exactly what the camp was. At least it didn't look like a refugee from a high school production of *South Pacific*, like most of Charlie's camps Gerber had seen. The communist soldiers here in the north might not be any more alert than they had been in Cambodia, and certainly less so than in South Vietnam, but they at least looked military, and so did their camp.

What Gerber couldn't see, however, and desperately wanted to see, was something, anything, that looked like it might possibly be a guardhouse, or even just a storeroom with a sturdy door where a prisoner might be kept locked up in. Gerber assumed such a structure would be readily identifiable by the presence of an armed guard outside it, but none was in evidence.

"I can't see a damned thing in there that looks like a cell," he whispered to Team Sergeant Fetterman who was lying beside him, his hands firmly gripping a suppressed Swedish K submachine gun. "I wish to hell we had one of those new Starlight gizmos."

Both men had heard rumors of a recently developed, passive night-viewing device and weapon sight that was supposed to enable the user to see in the dark by amplifying existing light from stars, the moon, or other sources, including the incandescence given off by rotting jungle vegetation. They had been provided with an active infrared viewing device and light source of British manufacture for the mission, but the night scope had proved unreliable and had failed to work after being only mildly jolted by Gerber's impact on the drop zone.

Fetterman carefully handed the silenced submachine gun to Gerber and studied the camp through his own binoculars. One man always kept an alert watch while the other observed the camp, in order to keep from being surprised by an enemy patrol. The remainder of the Americans, along with Bao, were deployed in a tight, defensive circle, fifteen meters back under the thicket.

The team had arrived within sight of the NVA camp where Jessup was believed to be incarcerated just before dawn. Without a thorough recon of the camp to determine exactly where Jessup was being held, a dawn raid was out of the question. Besides, with so small a force of men, Gerber had to be absolutely sure of the disposition of the NVA defenses. Even then, only extraordinary circumstances, such as an attempt to transfer Jessup, could warrant a daylight assault. The Green Berets would need the cover of darkness to break contact and throw off pursuit. Over Wilson's protests, Gerber had scotched the notion of any immediate action, and they had spent the day resting and studying the NVA garrison below.

Because of the impossibility of getting Bao to a doctor, at least until they could rendezvous with the naval forces that would be waiting off the coast at Mo Ron, McMillan had given Bao another shot of morphine and set the break in the tribesman's leg. Lacking plaster bandages, he had then improvised a cast from clay and mud from a nearby stream, reinforcing it with makeshift splints of bamboo. The end result had been an ungainly but effective mass that immobilized the break. Since it had been a simple fracture, and the skin had not been broken, there was little danger of infection from the teeming microorganisms in the mud and clay.

Other than that, there had been nothing they could do, except wait, and watch, and try to survive the heat of the day. Until now.

"You know, Master Sergeant, I've been thinking about how we're going to do this," said Gerber. "We've seen no sign of Jessup, and we've got to know exactly where he is before we hit this place. Which means we're going to have to get somebody in there to recon the place for us."

"Yes, sir. That would seem to be indicated by the situation," replied Fetterman.

"Now, I had planned to use Lieutenant Bao for

that, since, although he doesn't look like a Vietnamese, there are quite a few Tai tribesmen in this area, particularly Nung Tai, and I figured he'd attract less unwanted attention than a six-foot-tall Caucasian.''

''Yes sir. A low profile could be pretty important to whoever had to go in there.''

''But I can't send Bao in there because he's got a broken leg. He's been walking on it, and I've let him when I shouldn't have, but we were falling so far behind schedule that I had to. Still, he'd be practically helpless in a close fight.''

''Yes sir. That wouldn't do at all if he had to take out a sentry quietly.''

''So the problem is: I've got to find someone else to do the job.''

''Yes sir. I can see where that could be a problem, sir.''

Gerber sighed. ''The man I pick has got to be expert enough at covert operations and concealment to be able to get in and out of there undetected.''

''Yes sir.''

''And he's got to be close enough to the right size for a Vietnamese, in case someone spots him.''

''Yes sir.''

''And he's got to be expert enough at sentry removal and hand-to-hand combat to handle any unpleasantness that might come up.''

''Yes sir.''

''And he's got to be brave enough and tough enough to do the job.''

''Yes sir.''

''And one more thing.''

''What's that sir?''

"He's got to be crazy enough to try it. I'm sorry, Tony. I know you don't speak Vietnamese. And I know you've got more to go home for than the rest of us. Get ready. You're going down there in fifteen minutes."

"Yes sir."

Fetterman crawled into the thicket, found Bocker, and sent him out to maintain a guard with Gerber. Then he crawled over to where Tyme lay with the machine gun and the packs and radio.

"What's up?" Tyme asked as Fetterman began rummaging through his pack.

"Just going to take a little stroll down to the camp and see if I can spot our boy, Boom-Boom. Nothing to get excited about."

"B-U-L-L shit. Let me get Smith on this MG and I'll go with you."

"Negative, Boom-Boom. Not this time. You make more noise than a wandering buffalo when you go stomping around in those size-twelve clodhoppers of yours. This job calls for stealth, skill, and daring. Qualities in which you, my lad, are sadly lacking. Seriously, Boom-Boom, it really is a one-man operation. Besides, I want you on that RPD to cover my tail feathers if something goes wrong and I have to beat a hasty retreat across that damned open field down there."

"I still think I ought to go with you."

"Doesn't matter what you think, or what I think, for that matter. That's the way it's got to be. Here give me a hand with this thing, will you?"

Fetterman pulled his poncho and blanket roll from

the pack and spread it out on the ground, revealing a black, one-piece uniform with an attached hood and face mask that had been rolled up inside the bundle. The thing seemed to have innumerable bumps and bulges, but Tyme could not readily discern any pockets, or for that matter, any zippers or buttons. How one would put the costume on was a mystery.

"What in hell is that thing?" asked Tyme.

"Ninja suit," said Fetterman matter-of-factly. "My old scoutmaster always taught that it pays to be prepared."

"Since when are we issued Ninja suits for sterile operations? And while you're at it, what's a Ninja?"

"Since I bought this one in Japan, along with five others, way back during Korea, don't worry: it's sanitary. The Ninja were once a powerful guild of warriors and assassins in feudal Japan. They were experts at all kinds of martial arts, concealment, and infiltration. They were said to practice the art of invisibility. Their history contains many well-documented cases of Ninja masters who were supposed to have vanished in front of reliable witnesses. Many of their techniques are still practiced in the Korean martial art form known as Hwarang Do, but the Ninja themselves are supposed to be extinct."

"Supposed to be?"

"Well"—Fetterman grinned—"there's still me. Any other foolish questions?"

Tyme chuckled. "Just one. Were you really a Boy Scout?"

"Of course. Made Eagle before I was thirteen."

"Of course," said Tyme sourly.

*　　　*　　　*

"Ready to go, sir," said Fetterman.

"Christ, Sergeant, what're you wearing?"

"Ninja suit, sir. I, ah, already explained it to Sergeant Tyme. It's sterile, sir, and I've found it useful in the past for this kind of thing. Considering the circumstances, I didn't think you'd mind."

"It's results I need, Master Sergeant. The method I'll leave up to you."

"Thank you, sir. I'll try to be back in two hours."

As Fetterman started to move off, Gerber laid a restraining hand on his shoulder.

"Where's your weapon?"

"Left the K and the rest of my gear with Sergeant Tyme for the time being, sir. Compact as it is, the K's a little unhandy for this kind of work. A little flashy too."

"You're taking just a knife, then?"

"Course not, sir. Oh, I've got a knife all right. Couple of them. Got lots of little nasty tricks packed away in this Sunday-go-to-meetin' of mine. Knives are always quieter than guns. Just in case things go to shit on me in there, though, I've got this."

Fetterman's hand disappeared briefly though an invisible slit in his black night-fighter suit, and reappeared holding what looked like an overgrown semi-automatic pistol with a long silencer screwed onto the barrel. Although he had never actually seen one before, Gerber had seen photographs of the weapon, and recognized it as a Czechoslovakian-manufactured Vz61 machine pistol. Using the diminutive .32 ACP cartridge, the weapon made up in volume for what it lacked in punch. If Gerber recalled correctly, the gun had a cyclic rate of 950 rounds per minute when fitted with a silencer. Fetterman had taped three twenty-round magazines together, end to end.

"Sergeant, what in hell are you doing with a Skorpion?"

"Picked it up on a little side trip to Africa a few years ago, sir. Don't think I can say more than that. Besides, what else would one of Crinshaw's hand-picked nasty Scorpions use?"

Gerber shook his head. The one thing he had learned to expect from his unorthodox team sergeant in the few short weeks he had known him was the unexpected. "I'd rather not think of Crinshaw or his alliteration happy news team just now." He clapped Fetterman's shoulder again and squeezed the man's free hand briefly. "Good luck, you renegade Apache. And hurry back."

"Aztec, sir. Apache is what you had in the Old West. We've been Aztec for centuries."

"With a name like Fetterman?"

The master sergeant shrugged. "Well, nobody's perfect." He was lost to Gerber's sight before he had taken a half-dozen steps.

Fetterman lay in the tall grass, smelling the rank soil beneath him as he timed the roving guard on his endless circuit around the camp. The NVA soldier didn't seem to be following any schedule except that dictated by sloth. Fetterman selected the least well-lighted section of the fence, waited until the man had passed, then slithered forward. He examined the fence minutely, satisfied himself that it was neither electrified nor alarmed. Taking a small pair of wire cutters from a concealed pocket of his suit, he wrapped a bit of cloth about a small section of the bottom two wires to muffle the noise and clipped them in two. Then he slid soundlessly under the fence, returned the cutters to their hidden pocket, and carefully taped the wires back into place with small pieces of electrical tape.

Fetterman moved quietly across five meters of open ground and came up against the back of a small wooden building that was in heavy shadow, since it faced away from most of the lights in the camp. He remained there motionless for a minute, listening for any sounds, before checking further. Finally, having heard nothing, the Green Beret slid underneath the building and crept forward.

Nearly all the buildings in the camp were set from one to two feet above the ground, on wooden piles, in order to keep out snakes, rodents, and insects, as well as the runoff from the torrential rains common during the monsoon season. Fetterman considered the possibility that he might be crawling into a small, confining space already occupied by a cobra or banded krait, a bubonic-plague-carrying rat, or any of the numerous venomous insects endemic to Indochina, wished he hadn't, and, pushing the consideration from his mind, crawled on.

At the front of the building, he paused again to listen, but could hear only the distant chatter of the camp's diesel generator. It occurred to him, with mild surprise, that here in North Vietnam, which had enjoyed at least some limited industrial development under the French colonial government, he had expected electricity to be provided by normal power transmission lines. Apparently, as in South Vietnam, not all rural areas had been electrified. As he stared out from beneath the plank floor of the building, he could see a large wooden building to one side and a smaller building a few meters away. From the appearance of a number of storage tanks and outside basins, he deduced that the smaller building was either a bathhouse or laundry.

Through the gap between the bathhouse and the larger building, Fetterman could make out the corner of one of the long wooden barracks, although he could not see the watchtower he knew must stand in the open space between the barracks and the bathhouse. Earlier in the day he had observed that the camp had six of the long, thatched-roof structures, each of which appeared capable of holding twenty or thirty men, although only half had appeared in use. Evidently, either the remainder of the garrison had been relocated, or they were out doing something. Perhaps they were looking for the Green Berets. Fetterman hoped they were merely on training maneuvers, preferably in northern China.

Moving cautiously out from under the building, he rose quietly and glanced into the unlighted interior through an open window. Although his eyes were well adjusted to the darkness, it was difficult to make out anything inside the building in detail. At last he noticed two vaguely familiar shapes set against one wall of the single large room. It took him several seconds to recognize the objects for what they were: old fashioned, treadle-powered sewing machines. This was evidently the tailor shop, and that was not good news. For the NVA garrison to have such facilities, it would have to house at least a full company in strength, and probably more. Fetterman revised his estimate of the number of men each barrack could hold, and decided that the camp must be a battalion headquarters. That was too many NVA soldiers. Too damn many.

Next Fetterman checked the large building. Although constructed of finished lumber with a metal roof, it had only one shuttered window and a single, large wooden door, which was padlocked. He decided it was probably the supply building.

He edged slowly around the end of the supply shed and backed up quickly. Ahead were a half-dozen small frame structures with canvas tops. They reminded Fetterman of the squad tents the U.S. Army had used in World War II and Korea. A few of the tents had lightbulbs on inside them, and he could see soldiers inside through the screened windows. They were playing cards. Although most were wearing undershirts, a few had on uniform shirts, and from the rank insignia sewn on the shirts, he identified them as NVA sergeants. He had almost walked headlong into the NCO quarters.

Easing soundlessly under the corner of the supply building, Fetterman studied the situation. To the left, toward the center of the camp, was a large open area, the watchtower, then the barracks and parade ground. There was no cover at all. Beyond the NCO tents was the noisy generator shed and a large concrete building that would undoubtedly be the administration building. To get to it, he would either have to crawl between the tents where the men were playing cards or risk the small open area between the tents and the fence. That area was partially illuminated by a light atop a wooden pole outside the generator shed. He had lost track of the roving guard outside the wire.

Swearing silently to himself, in a variety of languages, he inched forward on his stomach between the tents. He was almost through the area when the screen door at the back of the last tent creaked noisily open on its rusty hinges, throwing a trapezoid of light across the grass directly in front of him.

Reacting instantly, Fetterman palmed out a West German paratrooper's knife with a gravity blade. He did not open it, but held it ready in his hand and mentally prepared himself to spring up from the ground and kill the man he knew must surely be about to exit the door. Then, instead of attacking or seeking cover, he froze where he was, even lowering his face to the ground, so that no light would fall on the tiny area of exposed skin between hood and mask that allowed him to see. It was a calculated risk, but there was no time for anything else.

Fetterman heard something shouted from inside the tent, in high-pitched singsong Vietnamese, but it didn't seem to have a quality of alarm about it. It was followed by a grunt from the partially open doorway that evoked a burst of laughter from those still playing cards inside.

He almost jumped when he felt something warm and wet hit his hand. Then a familiar, acrid aroma reached his nostrils.

I'll be a ringtailed son of a bitch, he thought. The dirty bastard is taking a leak on me!

A rash recruit probably would have reacted to such

a humiliating experience by assaulting the man. Fetterman, battle-hardened and professional, amused himself instead by silently imagining all the inventive things he might do to the communist soldier if he ever met him under other circumstances.

When the man finished urinating, he belched loudly, eliciting more laughter from inside, and returned to the card game. Fetterman wiped his hand and forearm through the grass, and hurried on.

The next phase was potentially the most dangerous. The concrete administration building was backed by the camp's generator shed, along with another building that contained what was obviously the base radio shack and, apparently, an operations center. The area was well lighted. The administration building fronted on an open area that appeared to be a parade ground or exercise yard, and was easily observable from the watchtower situated near the camp's center. The building itself, of poured concrete, sat directly upon the ground, making it impossible to crawl underneath. Careful observation, however, revealed a low band of shadow cast by the overhanging eaves of the building, along its front, extending upward from the ground a distance of about eight inches. Moving with the utmost care, Sergeant Fetterman was able to traverse the distance in about ten minutes of very slow crawling.

The Green Beret reconnoitered the building as best he could without actually going inside, then checked out the next structure, a padlocked, solidly built wooden building with only one entrance and no windows, which, he surmised, was the base armory. The door to the building was of riveted steel. It was certainly secure enough to serve as a cell for the missing U-2 pilot, but if it was the base armory—and no other building seemed to fit the bill—Jessup certainly wouldn't be locked up in there, where he'd have complete access to a large assortment of weapons.

Fetterman skirted a group of three small huts with tin roofs; like the administration building, they were made of concrete. They seemed to be officers' quarters. Although two were dark, Fetterman could see a man reading at a small desk in the third. All had screen doors, which made them unlikely candidates for a guardhouse.

Next he worked his way slowly around the mess hall and kitchen. No help there. No lights or activity either. Just a mixed bag of lingering smells: fish, rice, cabbage, that God-awful nouc-mam, and something that vaguely reminded Fetterman of scorched pumpkin pie.

There didn't seem to be anything left but the motor pool and the barracks area, neither of which seemed very likely places for detaining an important prisoner. Or an unimportant one for that matter. Still, one ought to check out all the possibilities, and Gerber had said he wanted a thorough recon of the place.

Fetterman would never have admitted it, not even to himself, but the truth of the matter was that he rather enjoyed sneaking around right under the noses of a large NVA garrison.

He pulled up the sleeve of his black night-fighter suit, and checked the luminous dial of his Hamilton watch. He had told Gerber he'd try to be back in two hours. He'd now used up ninety five minutes and found not the slightest sign that Jessup had ever been in the camp. Either the information they had was faulty or the man had already been moved. There was nothing further to be gained by crawling around inside the enemy camp. Nothing at all. Except the motor pool and the barracks. And it didn't seem possible that Jessup could be in either of those places. No way.

Fetterman pulled his sleeve back down to cover the watch and crawled, with infinite patience, across the open stretch of ground between the guard at the main gate and the watchtower until he reached the protective shadow of the maintenance shop at the edge of the motor pool.

The motor pool wasn't much to look at. There was a single GAZ field car, the Russian idea of what a jeep should look like, and four old Zil trucks, Russian-made copies of the American six-by-six two-and-a-half-ton truck that seemed to have been used or copied by just about everybody since the Second World War. Fetterman made mental note of the number and exact location of the vehicles as a matter of course. If the Americans hit the camp, which now seemed a remote possibility, it would be vital to destroy the enemy's means of rapid transport, in order to slow down pursuit. Fetterman was almost ready to leave when he noticed the motorcycle. Curious, he crawled forward for a closer look, expecting one of the Hondas that seemed to fill the streets in Saigon. He couldn't have been more wrong. The motor bike was an ancient, but evidently serviceable American-made model. He stared disbelievingly at the time-worn Harley-Davidson logo on the bike's fuel tank for several seconds before he crept away.

The brief delay probably saved the master sergeant's life. Had he left without noticing the motorcycle, he would have been completely exposed in the open area between the motor pool and the fuel storage area when it happened. As it was, he was still in the shadowed area of the maintenance shed when three armed NVA soldiers walked around the corner of it. The leader of the group stared him straight in the face.

Fetterman didn't hesitate. He took two steps forward and kicked the man viciously in the solar plexus, knowing a kick to the groin would have taken too long to have had the desired effect. As the man bent forward with a startled groan, Fetterman took one more step and snaked his left arm around the man's neck in a deadly embrace. Then he drove his right hand sharply forward, wrist locked. His palm caught the NVA soldier under the chin, snapping his head back and breaking his neck. A follow-up smash with a closed fist to the man's Adam's apple crushed his trachea, ensuring that the job wasn't left half finished.

Fetterman spun the dead soldier away from him with his left hand while his right moved back with lightning speed, disappeared in his clothing, then flicked forward like a striking rattlesnake. The second NVA trooper staggered backward amid choking, guttural sounds, a razor-sharp shuriken embedded in the hollow of his throat.

The third soldier had opened his mouth to yell a warning as he brought up his AK-47. Fetterman stepped away from the line of the weapon, wrapped his right arm about the communist soldier's, and used his left hand to force the AK abruptly on up and out against the fulcrum of his arm. He heard the satisfying sound of multiple cracks as the man's fingers, wrist, and elbow broke, then he slid his hand forward along the rifle and clamped his fingers firmly over the enemy's nose and mouth before he could scream in pain. Fetterman's right hand released the now-shattered arm, and his fingers found the German paratrooper knife. He thumbed the release. The blade dropped out and locked into place with a muffled snick as he twisted the soldier's head to one side. He drove the blade in just behind the man's left ear, twisted it, pulled out, and struck again, scrambling the NVA's brains.

Fetterman rolled off the dead soldier and right on top of the second one, driving the blade up under the rib cage and through the man's heart and one lung. The thrust was not necessary to kill the man. The shuriken had already done that, destroying both his wind pipe and jugular. But he had been making a noisy production out of dying. Fetterman's final stab put a swift, silent stop to his performance.

Fetterman came up quickly, the paratrooper knife ready to stab, slash, or be thrown if necessary, but there was no further threat. The entire fight had been amazingly quiet, and had lasted just over five seconds. Had any of the three men succeeded in yelling or firing a weapon, Fetterman would have been up to his belt bucklet in NVA soldiers. As it was, no one in the camp seemed to have noticed the disturbance, except of course for the three dead men, who would tell no tales.

The Green Beret sergeant quickly checked the immediate area to make certain there were no additional enemy soldiers present and then hid the bodies in the only location that presented itself: beneath a tarpaulin in the back of one of the Zil trucks. With luck, they would remain undiscovered, at least until morning. It wasn't much time, but it would have to be enough. Anywhere else in the camp would be even more obvious. By the time the bodies were found, Fetterman planned to be several miles away, moving fast in rough country. By the time the NVA mobilized an effective search and found the American's trail, it would be a very cold one, even with Bao's leg and that blundering Wilson slowing them down.

The one fault in that plan, Fetterman knew, was that there was no way of telling how soon the men might be missed and a search for them instituted. Three armed soldiers moving about at this time of the night obviously weren't just out taking a stroll. If they were an internal roving guard, their absence would be noted when they failed to report in. If they had been an intended relief for the posted sentries at the gate, in the tower, and outside the fence, their absence would be noticed immediately by the men they were to replace, but might well go unreported until the next watch. Particularly if the sentries assumed their fellow privates were goofing off and did not wish to get them into trouble with the sergeant of the guard. If they had just been relieved themselves, they might go unnoticed until roll call. Fetterman could not bank on that. It was time to go.

Remembering the advice given by Major Robert Rogers to his rangers during the French and Indian War—never take the same route home, and you won't get ambushed—Sergeant Fetterman opted to cut through the fence at the edge of the drill field, behind the fuel storage shed. He would tape the wires back together to temporarily hide his exit, as he had when he entered the far side of the camp, then move into the treeline and work his way back around to Gerber and the rest of the team on the ridge line to the west. It was going to make him a good forty-five minutes late getting back, but seemed like a safer idea than trying to work his way back through the enemy camp.

As he crawled toward the fence, Fetterman became aware of a faint odor in the air. The night air was filled with myriad smells, from the jungle, the nearby canal, the camp itself. There was the scent of the soil, and of raw sewage, and the lingering traces of leftovers from the evening meal mixed in with the smells of grease and oil and gasoline from the motor pool, not to mention his own sweat. But there was something else too: a vague, faintly fragrant aroma that was somehow familiar. The Special Forces sergeant couldn't identify the brand, but he would have bet a week's pay against a fish head that it was some kind of expensive French men's cologne.

So intent was Fetterman upon locating the source of the smell that he almost fell into the hole. A rapid examination indicated that he would not have fallen far, however. The touch of his hands revealed that the hole, about four feet square, was crisscrossed by steel bars set in concrete, with a small, double-padlocked trapdoor in the middle of the grate.

Fetterman fished a small pen light out of his ninja suit. One end of the light was wrapped in red plastic. Cupping a black-gloved hand around the front of the light to direct its beam downward, he closed one eye and briefly flicked the switch on, then off again. In the second and a half that the dim light illuminated the bottom of the pit, Fetterman could see a blind-folded, handcuffed, and shackled man, wearing only a pair of undershorts, trying unsuccessfully to accommodate his five-foot ten-inch frame, to the four-foot floor space below.

It was Jessup.

CHAPTER 6 ———————————

"Well, sir, that's pretty much the layout of the place," said Fetterman as he finished sketching a diagram of the camp onto the large sheet of paper with a grease pencil. "Our boy is located right about here, in the concrete pit, with a set of steel bars over the top of him. The cage isn't really big enough to lie down or stand up in. At least, I'm pretty sure it's our boy. It's a Caucasian anyway. Given the circumstances, I thought it best not to tell him I was there."

"You mean you didn't even tell him we're here?" interrupted Wilson. "You didn't even let the man know we've come to rescue him? I'm sorry, but I just don't understand how you could do that. The man must feel that all hope is lost. Think what just a few words from you could have done for his spirit. But then, I don't understand why you didn't bring him out with you, if it was so easy to get in and out, if he had no guards as you say."

Fetterman stared icily at Wilson, his face an unreadable mask in the eerie light cast by the red plastic lenses over the men's flashlights.

"No, Wilson, you don't understand. If you did, you wouldn't ask such stupid questions," said Gerber. "Sergeant Fetterman couldn't bring Jessup out with him because he didn't have anything to cut through the lock or the cage bars or the handcuffs or the leg irons with. It takes more than a pair of wire cutters for that kind of cutting, and it also makes a lot of noise. Now I'm sure making a lot of noise doesn't sound very important to you, especially since that's practically the only thing you've done since we started this mission, but it's an important consideration to a lone soldier like Sergeant Fetterman here, who happens to find himself in the middle of an enemy camp surrounded by a battalion of NVA soldiers, any one of which would be only too glad to shoot the good sergeant full of holes with an AK-47. Which is also precisely why Sergeant Fetterman didn't speak to Jessup. Even had it been safe enough to whisper something to the man, which I sure as hell wouldn't have done under the circumstances, there would be no way to predict how Jessup might have reacted to suddenly hearing an American voice say, 'Take it easy, buddy, we've come to get you out.'

"Suppose he'd thought it was some kind of NVA trick and started swearing at Master Sergeant Fetterman. Or suppose he'd been so happy he shouted with joy. Then we'd have two men down there to rescue, and the whole damned camp, not to mention every soldier in North Vietnam with access to a radio, alerted to the fact that the rest of us were out here. And as for ease of getting in and out, it seems to me you're forgetting the little matter of the three soldiers Sergeant Fetterman had to kill. Don't worry, Wilson, we'll get your precious little flyboy out of there for you, but we'll do it our way, which means we'll do it right. Then, maybe, just maybe, if we're really very lucky, just maybe none of us will get killed in the process, Wilson. Not even you.''

Dismissing Wilson without even so much as a wave of the hand, he turned back to Fetterman. ''Okay, Master Sergeant. Let's have your recommendations on how to take this place.''

''Well sir, like I was saying, it isn't going to be easy. I don't think the problem's so much going to be the guards as it is all the people we're going to wake up once things start popping. Indications are that this place is a battalion HQ. They must have at least a full company of men down there, and at least another full company out in the boonies somewhere. Maybe they're trail watching, maybe they're picking rice, maybe they're looking for us. I don't know where they are, and that's what really worries me, because if they have a radio, and I wouldn't want to bet they don't, all those guys down there have to do is make one little radio call to let their buddies know which direction we're headed, and we could find ourselves between the proverbial rock and a hard place.''

''You're right,'' Gerber nodded. ''We'll never be lucky enough to get Jessup out without somebody hearing us and sounding the alarm. That sort of textbook-perfect operation only happens in textbooks. We'll have to hit the whole camp, destroy the radio transmitter, and hope they don't have backup, and create the maximum amount of panic and confusion possible. Then we'll try to spring Jessup and get ourselves out of there under cover of all the noise. You concur?''

"Affirmative, sir. I would suggest we go in quiet, get set up so we can spring Jessup as soon as the shooting starts. Then we get very noisy, and once the place is good and loud, we get very quiet and run away.''

"That's it?'' said Wilson sarcastically. "That's your whole plan?''

"More or less." Fetterman smiled.

"Wilson"—Gerber sighed—"will you please just shut up and listen for once. Give it a try just this once, for me, will you? You might actually learn something.''

Gerber was having an increasingly difficult time tolerating Wilson's constant interruptions and showboating. The man made more noise than a herd of wounded moose moving through dry brush, he seemed to have almost no knowledge of field craft, and it had never been fully explained what his function was on the mission. Besides which, he had wanted to abandon Bao when the tribesman broke his leg during a bad PLF at the drop zone. Wilson had also called Bao a gook. Gerber didn't give a damn if Mr. Super Spook from the CIA was the Grand Imperial Wizard of the triple K in Virginia, but by God he would not tolerate that kind of racist shit on a combat patrol. Bao was a trusted ally and a damned fine soldier, and Wilson was going to treat him as such or Gerber would personally tromp Mr. Wilson's civilian hotshot ass into the ground.

"Okay," Gerber continued, "here's the way I see

it. We've got about nine targets to hit, and only eight men. Number one, we've got to take out the watch-tower in the center of the camp. The master sergeant here says there's a light machine gun in it, probably an RPD. The guy in the tower is in an exposed position, but he's also in a position to make things very miserable for anybody caught out in the open, inside or outside the camp. Number two, the radio shack. That's got to be blown in order to keep them from getting out a call for help or organizing a pursuit. Same goes for number three, the motor pool. If we take away their wheels, they can't run any faster than we can. Target four is Jessup. He's why we're here, after all. If we could slip him out quietly, we could ignore most of the rest. From what Master Sergeant Fetterman says, however, we're going to have to blow the lock off his cage.''

He pointed to Smith. ''Sully, that's a job for some of that plastique of yours.

''That only leaves us with the NCO quarters and the officers' quarters, which, if we could do a little house cleaning there, might make getting the troops organized just a bit complicated for our NVA friends down there. And the armory, which we'd be foolish not to hit. And the generator shack, which would be a nice plus, as well as knocking out the lights and making getting organized just that much tougher on Charlie.

''Okay guys, that's the good news. Now then, I'm open to ideas. Anybody want to make a suggestion as to how we ought to do this thing, besides the basics already offered by Sergeant Fetterman? Keep in mind that aside from a handful of AKs and some grenades, we've got one MG and one RPG to do it with.''

"Sir, if I may?" said Bocker.

"Go ahead, Sergeant."

"We're going to have to cross a lot of open ground going into and coming out of that place. Going in, we'll presumably be quiet enough not to attract too much attention. Coming out, they're going to know we've been there. The fact that we haven't seen mortars or other machine guns doesn't mean they don't have them. Particularly on a camp this size. I think it might be wise if we were to position our machine gun so as to provide covering fire during the exfiltration. Although manning the MG is a two-man job, one man can handle it, and since Lieutenant Bao has a bad leg anyway, it would seem logical to site him somewhere along the ridge here, with the RPD."

"Good point, Galvin. Anybody else?"

"Well, sir," said Fetterman, "the NCO set up is just a bunch of squad tents, and the officers' quarters are concrete, but only closed by screen doors, which ought to make them ideal grenade targets. I would think that two men at each location, possibly three for the NCO area simply because of the greater number of targets, would be sufficient to handle the situation in those locales. The team hitting the NCO tents would have to neutralize the watchtower first, and could accomplish demolition of the generator afterward. Those men tasked to destroy the officers' quarters should be able to set a couple of charges underneath the armory before clearing the area. It wouldn't be a proper job, but it should cause some damage to the contents of the building, and if any

ammunition or explosions are stored there, we could
get very lucky indeed. I didn't spot any bunkers for
ammo or explosives during the recon.''

"Thank you, Master Sergeant. I believe those are
solid suggestions. However, it seems to me that
we've got to knock out the radio room at practically
the instant this show starts, or we run the risk of the
enemy being able to call for reinforcements.''

"Sir, if I may," Fetterman continued. "We've got
a couple of willy pete grenades. If I could get into
the proper position, I could toss one of them into the
radio shack to initiate the action, while Sergeant
Tyme covered the officers' quarters. The place is
wooden, and ought to burn well. I don't think anyone
would have time to get a message out. I could use
two grenades for an added measure of safety, then
immediately join Sergeant Tyme in neutralizing the
officers. We could then proceed to accomplish the
demolition of the suspected armory. The whole thing
should take a minute and a half, two minutes at
most.''

"I would prefer to have you with the team sent to
extract Major Jessup, since you know his exact
location.''

"I took that into consideration, sir. I don't believe
the rescue team will have any trouble locating the
major's cell. Also, blowing the lock without injuring
the major is clearly a job that Sergeant Smith is more
qualified than myself to perform. I believe he should
be accompanied by Sergeant McMillan, in case the
major is in need of medical attention. At that point,
we're beginning to spread ourselves pretty thin, so
Sergeant Tyme and I seem a logical choice for the

officers/armory/radio shack part of it. That would leave Sergeant Bocker, Mr. Wilson, and yourself to neutralize the watchtower, NCOs, and the generator, and try to keep the troops busy. The sergeant is handy with an RPG, I believe, and should initiate the raid by taking out the watchtower. After that, he could use the remaining rounds on the barracks. Given the way they're sited—four in front lengthwise with two across the back—he ought to be able to hit all of them, even without indirect fire capability. Sergeant Bocker is cross trained in light weapons and is familiar with the RPG-7. Sergeant Tyme and I are both familiar with basic demolitions, and we've worked well together before. Since we're going to have lots of things to do, and little time to do them in, I prefer to have him with me, with your permission, sir. Also, I assume you'll want the main radio with you, and Sergeant Bocker is the commo expert.''

"How about it, Sergeant Bocker? Think you can do the job?'' Gerber asked.

"No sweat, sir.'' The big sergeant grinned. "I just love making things go bang. Not as much as Sergeant Smith, but almost. And when you've got an RPG, well, long distance is the next best thing to being there.''

"All right. That's the way we'll break up the team then. Master Sergeant, I thought you said the radio shack had screen wire over the windows. How do you propose to get a grenade inside?''

Fetterman held up a machete. "The radio shack isn't too high off the ground, sir. One good swipe with this thing, at the rear window, ought to give me all the room I'll need to get a couple of grenades inside.''

Gerber turned to the man from Langley.

"Mr. Wilson, once things start popping in there, an awful lot is going to depend on each man doing his job exactly as ordered, without hesitation or argument. How about it, do you think you can give Sergeant Bocker and me a hand in dealing with those NCO tents? If you can do just that much, we can take care of the rest, but it won't be easy without your help."

Wilson considered the obvious objection that he ought to go with the rescue team in order to be able to debrief Jessup as soon as possible about the fate of the U-2, but given the number of targets that it would be necessary to neutralize and how few men they had available for each task, he could see the logic of deploying them as Fetterman and Gerber had suggested.

"I'm no commando, Captain, but I've been in a few shoot-outs in my day. I can handle this AK reasonably well, and I know how to throw a grenade. I'll hold up my end of things. I told you back in Saigon that the tactical part of this mission was your show. You just tell me what to do, and I'll do it."

"Thank you," said Gerber with some surprise. He had more than halfway expected an argument from the CIA man.

"All right. As I see it, we're going to have to enter the camp from three locations. The main assault team will enter the camp through the wire at Sergeant Fetterman's initial entry point, after eliminating the roving guard. Sergeant Fetterman and Sergeant Tyme will then cut the wire in back of the armory, enter the camp, and proceed to a position where they can effectively neutralize their targets. The rescue team will have to neutralize the guard at the front gate without being observed from the watchtower. They will then proceed to a position outside the fence opposite the motor pool, cut through the wire there, contact Jessup, and effect his rescue. After rescuing the major, the rescue team will demolish the POL dump and destroy such enemy transport as may be possible before exfiltrating from the camp with the major. The signal to commence firing will be when Sergeant Smith blows the major's cell open, or if the enemy discovers us and opens fire. If Sergeant Smith is unable to locate the cell or Jessup isn't in it, he will break radio silence using the walkie-talkie and contact Sergeant Bocker. Sergeant Bocker will have the backpack unit and I will be with him. I will then decide whether to continue with the raid or to terminate the mission and withdraw.''

Gerber turned to Smith. ''Sully, any problem with cracking open the major's cage?''

''There shouldn't be, sir. I will need the bolt cutters to take care of the handcuffs and shackles, sir, in case the Peerless keys won't fit. We won't have time to fool around with the manacles if it turns out Charlie doesn't use standard keys. From what Master Sergeant Fetterman says, the padlocks are too big for the cutters, but I have something I think will work just fine.''

''Okay, that's it then, unless somebody has something else.''

''Sir, if I may make a suggestion,'' said Smith.

''Go ahead, Sergeant.''

''Well sir, when the shit hits the fan, those NVA troops in the barracks are going to try to bug out.

Now, they're not going to come storming across open ground toward an RPG and a couple-three automatic weapons unless they're either incredibly brave or incredibly stupid. Especially if they aren't armed. But they might try to bug out the back or the sides and get to the armory or flank us.

"Now Master Sergeant Fetterman is going to solve the armory problem for us, assuming that we've guessed right about which building is the armory. I'll pre-rig three or four charges for him out of the French plastic explosive we brought along. But if things don't go right, or if they have their arms with them, we ought to have a backup plan in mind."

"Have you got an idea you'd like to share with us, Sergeant Smith?" asked Gerber.

"Well, sir, originally I'd recommend a few claymores to cover the north and east sides of the barracks, but given the number of men we've got and the difficulties in getting the mines properly sited, I don't think we can do much about that. I do, however, have an idea for taking care of the southern escape route, if we could figure some way of taking out the guy in the tower without making quite so much noise as an RPG round is going to make."

"Enlighten me," said Gerber.

"There are bound to be some jerry cans around the motor pool, sir," Smith continued. "Maybe even some on the trucks, already filled. If I could have ten minutes to work uninterrupted, after the man in the tower had been eliminated, I could string half a dozen claymores, about half of what we got with us, along the north side of the parade ground and put one or two five-gallon cans of gasoline in front of each one. The fence will pretty well hem in anyone trying to get out to the east. If they go north, I can't do much about it, but if they come south, toward the armory or motor pool, the combination of shrapnel and burning gasoline ought to make them reconsider the error of their ways. It could buy us several minutes of time and would provide a measure of protection for the rescue team extracting the major.''

''A commendable notion, Sully, but I don't see how we can accommodate you about the watchtower.''

''Sir,'' said Fetterman, ''I've a suggestion on that point. Back in Saigon, Mr. Wilson stressed my penchant for unusual weaponry. The Ninja suit wasn't the only non-issue item I brought along. Oh, we could just hose down the tower with one of the Ks or the Skorpion, but somebody might overhear, even quiet as they are. I've a takedown blow gun in my kit and half a dozen darts, coated with curare, guaranteed to cause death in about ten seconds. Paralysis should set in long before that. The darts are notched, so that the tip will break off below the skin, guaranteeing that the poison will have time to take effect before the dart can be removed. It's almost absolutely silent, and I can hit a man from thirty yards with it consistently.''

Gerber considered, then shook his head. ''It's no good, Tony. The closest cover has got to be forty-five, maybe fifty yards from the tower. Besides, timing is crucial. You've got to be sure of being in position to knock out that radio, and I can't shoot a blow gun.''

''I can shoot blow gun,'' said Bao quietly. ''Nung hunt with blow gun as long as there have been Nung.

Mostly use crossbow now, but nearly all Nung know how to use blow gun. All Nung men learn when little boy.''

"That's right, Captain," said Fetterman. "Many of the ethnic tribes of Indochina have hunted with blow guns. No one knows for sure how long.''

Gerber shook his head. "That still doesn't change the fact that the range is fifty yards. Besides, we need Bao on the RPD to cover our withdrawal.''

"How far is fifty yards?" asked Bao.

"A little less than forty-six meters," Fetterman told him. The tribesman was familiar with the metric system used by the American army and the French, who had ruled Indochina from the mid-nineteenth century to the mid-twentieth and left a strong influence on the region.

"Mmmm. That long shot," Bao agreed, "but I hit man from forty-six meters. I once kill tiger with blow gun from one hundred and seven steps. That about eighty meters.''

"If I may, Captain," interrupted Wilson before Gerber could object that such an attempt would still leave them with no one to cover their withdrawal. "Suppose, instead of destroying the trucks to slow down pursuit, we were to destroy all the trucks but one. We could use that truck to escape in. It should easily be able to crash the gate, or the fence for that matter. It would get us clear of the area in a hurry, and we could ditch it a mile or two down the road, before we have a chance to run into anyone else. The general confusion in the camp could eliminate the need for covering fire and give us a good head start.

I'll admit it's a bit cowboyish, but the approach does offer a number of advantages.''

Gerber still didn't like the idea. It went against the basic infantry tactics of fire and maneuver elements. Covering your withdrawal from a raid with supporting fire was standard army practice, but then, the Special Forces had never been famous for following standard army practice. He found himself wondering if he wasn't resisting the idea just because Wilson had thought of it. The idea was risky, but then so was using only eight men to hit an NVA camp garrisoned with at least an enemy company. The whole mission had been a risk from the very start, yet each of them had accepted the risk without hesitation.

"I don't know. We could be in a lot of trouble if Smith and McMillan can't get one of those trucks started," he said.

"Captain," said McMillan, getting into the act, "I think we can do it. We'll make sure we've got one of them running, then run a gasoline trail along the rest of them. A deuce-and-a-half doesn't need a key to start it, and Sergeant Fetterman said these are Russian copies of six-by's. Even if these do need a key, I can hot-wire one. Sully's improvised hot shrapnel bombs should give us all the time we need to get something running and help cover your team and Sergeant Fetterman's as you withdraw toward the motor pool. Even a second-class ride beats a first-class walk, sir. It's got to be better than trying to cross all that open ground outside the camp on foot.''

"Is that the way you all feel about it?" asked Gerber.

Tyme, who seldom had much to say, spoke up. "Hell, Captain. We all got the same guarantee we were born with. If something doesn't kill us, we'll live till we die."

"One thing," said Bao. "This long shot. Must have long blow gun, light darts, if plan to work. How long blow gun, Sergeant Tony?"

"Almost three meters assembled, Lieutenant. And the darts are bamboo, the lightest kind. It's a good rig."

Bao's teeth flashed briefly in the darkness. "Then we set," he said. "What you say, Captain Mack? Can do?"

"Okay, Bao, can do. Get organized, people. We move out in five minutes."

CHAPTER 7 _____

Fetterman killed the sentry.

It was a simple thing to do. As the rover walked past the Special Forces men concealed in the tall grass, Fetterman, still wearing the Ninja suit, rose silently from the ground, took two steps, and swung both hands back over his head, the handles of a piano-wire garrote clenched in his fists. Fetterman snapped his arms down, throwing the garrote over the sentry's head and pulling it rearward and down. As the wire bit into the man's throat, Fetterman drove his knee into his back and pulled him backward against this fulcrum. Then, bringing his elbows together, the Green Beret sergeant spun to the left, crossing the wire of the garrote over itself as he bent sharply forward at the waist, then straightened his legs, lifting the NVA trooper's feet clear of the ground. The wire cut deeply into the man's throat from bottom to top. Fetterman completed his movement by bringing the man on over on his head, in a throw designed to snap the neck, then finished the attack by driving a knee into the sentry's collarbone, snapping it, and pulling the garrote tight.

Except for the snapping of his neck and collarbone, the only sound the NVA trooper had made was a dull thud as he hit the wet grass.

Wilson, who had never seen a man actually garroted and had observed the attack from only a few feet away, fought hard to keep from being sick. The master sergeant's sudden, brutal attack had completely severed the enemy soldier's head.

Fetterman quickly dragged the body a few feet into the elephant grass, where it would be less likely to be discovered should anyone look, and relieved the corpse of its weapon. Then he showed Gerber the spot where he had entered the camp earlier. The location was shielded from observation from the watchtower by the back of the tailor shop and the front corner of the supply building.

After indicating the spot where the fence had been cut, Fetterman slipped back into the high grass with Sergeant First Class Tyme. The two men would work their way along the fence line, crawling slowly through the grass until they were at a point opposite the building believed to be the camp armory. They would then cut a new passage through the wire and come up behind the building, which would place them between the radio shack and the officers' quarters, their primary targets. Because the high grass offered some cover and the intervening buildings tended to partially obstruct the view from the watchtower, both Fetterman and Gerber believed that such a route would be safer than attempting to crawl through the NCO quarters as Fetterman had done earlier.

*   *   *

Meanwhile, McMillan and Smith, who had separated from the rest of the team when they were about halfway across the grassy field, had worked their way around to a position where they were within striking distance of the guard at the main gate, on the south side of the NVA camp. At that point, they could do nothing but wait, while McMillan listened through a tiny earplug to the static on the Telefunken-made walkie-talkie. When he heard the double pause in the background noise that would be caused by Bocker breaking squelch twice on the big backpack unit, he would signal Smith that the guard in the watchtower had been eliminated. Smith would then move forward and kill the gate guard. Until that time, however, he could not attack. The front-gate guard post was clearly visible from the tower.

As Wilson pressed himself tight against the back of the supply building, he noticed that he was sweating profusely. The night was warm, he told himself, but he knew that it wasn't all that warm. The wooden pistol grip and fore-end of the AK-47 were slippery in his hands, and the memory of the decapitated guard was sharp in his mind. He fully realized, for the first time since he had been given this mission back at Langley, that the odds were really quite good that he was going to die. He had never really faced death before. He had cheated it, tricked it, laughed his way out of it, but this time it was staring him right square in the face. He had the strangest feeling that if he blinked, he would never open his eyes again.

Behind Wilson, Sergeant Bocker was carefully laying high explosive grenades for the RPG-7 out on the ground in front of himself. When Bocker had six of the cone-shaped rocket-propelled grenades in a neat row, he inserted one of them into the launcher and removed the safety cap from the end of the grenade.

While Bocker readied the Soviet-made Grenade launcher, Gerber relieved Bao of the RPD machine gun and crouched near the corner of the supply building. He trained the muzzle of the gun on the nearest NCO tent, ready to fire instantly should the Special Forces men be discovered.

Bao, for his part, calmly screwed together the sections of Fetterman's blow gun, as the master sergeant had showed him how to do. When he had completed assembling the nine-foot-long weapon, he took it and the handful of poison darts and disappeared beneath the supply building.

Fetterman and Tyme had by now succeeded in penetrating the fence unobserved and were crouched in shadow in back of the armory. Tyme had slung his Swedish K around his neck so that it hung in front of his chest where it would be instantly available. He held a grenade in each hand. At a nod from Fetterman, he pulled both pins. Now only the safety levers prevented activation of the grenade fuses.

Fetterman, at the other corner of the building, partially straightened the pin on a white phosphorus grenade in a pocket attached to his ammunition pouches in order to make it easier to pull out the pin. Then he took a second WP grenade in his left hand, removed the pin, and drew his machete with his right hand. They were ready for Smith's signal.

Using his sapling crutch, Lieutenant Bao worked his way to the front right corner of the supply building and peered cautiously out from underneath. Except for the lone guard in the tower, there was no sign of anyone.

Bao carefully eased the blow gun out from beneath the building and inserted a dart in the rear of the tube. Fitting the mouthpiece carefully to his lips, he drew in a large lungful of air and huffed it out abruptly.

The shot was a complete miss.

Reloading the blow gun quickly, Bao fired again. The second dart struck the side of the tower with a sharp crack.

In the tower, the guard stepped to the side and bent over the wall to see what had struck it.

Bao's third dart hit the man in the back of the neck. The NVA soldier groped for the object that had struck him with his right hand, lost his grip on the railing with his left, and toppled headfirst to the ground with a sickening crunch.

The Nung tribesman scuttled back under the building, breaking down the blow gun as he crawled. He stuffed the weapon into his pack, then reclaimed the RPD from Gerber, who immediately unslung his own AK-47 as the Tai flashed him a quick grin.

"Third time is charm, Captain Mack. Northern Cong go down for long count."

"Third time?" queried Gerber.

"Take three darts. Miss with first two. Very sorry,

but I not familiar with Sergeant Tony's blow gun. Not know how much lung to use. Third time is charm, just like in movies. Northern Cong dead now.''

Gerber shot him an incredulous look but said nothing. He nodded to Bocker, who keyed his microphone switch twice, then picked up the RPG-7.

Gerber took two fragmentation grenades from his pistol belt and motioned for Wilson to do likewise, pointing to the two tents he wished the CIA man to throw a grenade into, then held up a restraining hand to remind the man to wait for Smith's signal.

McMillan had seen the guard fall from the tower, but had waited for Bocker's signal. When he heard the twin clicks, he reached into a pocket on his fatigue pants and brought out a handful of dirt and small pebbles he had collected earlier. Swinging his arm in a low arc, he flipped the handful of debris up against the side of the sentry box nearest the gate.

The NVA guard, who had been dozing on his feet, snapped awake as if he had been poked with an electric cattle prod. Unslinging his rifle, the guardsman stepped out of the sentry box and right into a hard-swung butt stroke from Sergeant Smith.

The butt of Smith's AK-47 caught the man squarely across the bridge of the nose, and the enemy soldier went down as if he had been pole-axed. A combat boot stomped into his throat and a bayonet thrust into his thorax ensured permanency of results.

With the gate guard dead and the threat from the tower eliminated, McMillan and Smith collected the sentry's weapon and ammunition, then simply opened the gate, which was not locked, entered the camp, closed the gate behind them, and made directly for the motor pool.

After a quick check of the motor pool and maintenance shop area to ascertain that no one was there, the two Green Berets moved immediately to the edge of the parade ground and located the underground cell that Fetterman had described to them. McMillan flicked his red-lensed flashlight briefly on and off. Somebody was in there all right.

"Jessup!" McMillan whispered hoarsely. "Are you Major Malcolm Jessup? We're U.S. Army Special Forces. We've come to get you out, man."

"Americans? You're American? I can't see. Those gook bastards blindfolded me. Oh, sweet mother of God, man. If you really are Americans, get me out of here before they come back."

"Be cool, man," said Smith. "And keep your voice down. You're going to wake up half of North Vietnam. Now get back in the corner and protect your face and ears if you can. We're going to have to blow the lock on this thing to get you out of there."

Smith turned to McMillan. "Check out the transportation, then see if you can scrounge up some full jerry cans. I can manage here. As soon as you can, get back here, and we'll set up the claymores before we blow this thing."

"Right."

While McMillan left to find a set of wheels and some gas cans, Smith tied a small amount of detonation cord about the shackle of each of the two padlocks securing the cage door and taped a non-electric blasting cap onto the end of the cord. He crimped the end of the cap to a short length of safety fuse and attached the fuse to an M-60 fuse lighter. By the time he had finished, McMillan was back, a five-gallon jerry can of gasoline in each hand.

"Great," said Smith. "Any more of those things back there?"

"Six all together," gasped McMillan.

At six and a half pounds to the gallon of gas, the two jerry cans had weighed in excess of sixty-five pounds, and he was already heavily burdened with pack, weapon, and medical kit.

"There was one apiece on each of the trucks and two on the jeep."

"Okay. Get the other four. I'll rig these up and keep an eye on our boy here."

"Making me the beast of burden, is it? Since when did I become the pack mule around here?"

"Since you forgot to get yourself cross-trained in demolitions, you big ox. Besides, I just heard you volunteer."

"Is that what that sound was? I thought it was me having a heart attack. I don't suppose you'd mind if I only carry them two at a time?"

"You'll just have to make an extra trip that way." Smith grinned. "But you go ahead. A man ought to do what he thinks is right."

"Thanks for reminding me," muttered McMillan as he lurched away.

"What's going on out there?" demanded Jessup. "Why don't you get me out of here?"

"Patience, Major, patience," soothed Smith, taping a claymore to the back of one of the jerry cans. "All things in good time, Major. You just keep hunkered down in that corner and keep you head down. We'll get you out of there okay."

"Well hurry up about it."

"Don't get pushy, Major. We might just go away."

"Problem?" asked McMillan, sliding up with two more jerry cans. He nodded briefly toward the pit.

Smith crimped another blasting cap onto a length of det-cord, inserted it into the detonator well of one of the claymores, and attached the other end of the cord to a second claymore in the same fashion.

"Nah. The Major's just worried we're having so much fun up here that we'll forget all about him and leave him down there. I've got the cage ready to blow. Just get me those other two gas cans, and we can get this show on the road."

Smith had finished rigging all four jerry cans when McMillan returned. "What kept you?" he asked anxiously. "I was starting to get worried."

He was serious.

"Almost forgot I needed to lay a gasoline trail over the vehicles. Had to use one of the cans, so I refilled it for you."

"Refilled it?" Smith's voice couldn't hide his amazement.

"Yeah. Damned gas pump was locked. That's what took me so long."

"Locked? How did you open it?"

"Didn't. Nozzle was padlocked to the tank. I just cut the hose and let the gas run out. We better move quickly, though, 'cause right now it's running all over the floor of Charlie's maintenance shop. When the motor pool goes up, old Charlie is going to lose his garage as well as his trucks."

Smith smiled. "You know, Doc, we just might make a demolitions man out of you yet."

While McMillan caught his breath and stood by to blow open the cell if necessary, Smith emplaced the flame expedients. He set four of the claymore and gasoline bombs in a row, tied them together with detonator cord, inserted an electric blasting cap in the end bomb, and ran the lead back to an M-57 firing device at the corner of the maintenance shop after testing the circuit. The other two jerry cans and claymores he placed about fifteen meters in front of the underground cell, linked them with det-cord, and rigged an M-1 pull firing device and a trip wire off each end.

"This way," explained Smith, "we get two cracks at Charlie. One when he tries to come across the parade ground and one when he comes to check the cell or put out the fires after we leave."

McMillan nodded vigorously to signify his comprehension and left to get the transportation ready. When Smith heard a truck start up in the motor pool, he called a final warning to Jessup and pulled the pin on the fuse lighter, then took five quick steps away from the cell and dropped flat.

The explosion that severed the padlocks on Jessup's cell was not loud, but in the stillness of the night it seemed awesome to Wilson. He felt his nerve slipping. He wanted to run and hide somewhere. Then he realized that Gerber was yelling at him, and he moved quickly forward, yanked open the door of the nearest squad tent, and tossed the fragmentation grenade inside.

Wilson had sense enough not to wait to see what happened with his grenade. He remember that much from the special tactics course they'd taught him at

Camp Perry. He ran a half-dozen steps to the second tent, ripped open the door, and tossed the second grenade inside. Then he took two quick steps away, dived underneath the supply building, and covered his ears as he heard the whoosh of Bocker firing the RPG-7.

At the sound of Smith's explosion, Sergeant First Class Tyme rose up from the shadows between two of the officers' huts, where he had been crouched. He jumped to the top step of one hootch, kicked in the bottom part of the screen door, and rolled a fragmentation grenade in on the floor. Tyme then leaped ahead to the second hut and drove his fist, grenade and all, through the bottom of the screen. He released the grenade, yanked out his hand, and rolled away from the building.

The two grenades exploded with tremendous effect inside the small, concrete structures, riddling the tin roofs with shrapnel. Tyme jumped backward, came up against the final hut, and tossed a third grenade inside before dropping to the ground alongside the concrete wall of the hootch. When the grenade went off, he scrambled back to his feet and dashed inside the hut, spraying the interior with 9mm bullets from his submachine gun. Then he ran from hut to hut, repeating his performance at each one, making sure the men inside were dead.

While Tyme was busy reducing the ranks of the NVA officer corps, Fetterman cut down on the size of its inventory of communications gear.

The instant the master sergeant heard the explosion

signifying Jessup's release, he stepped across the short space between the armory and the radio shack and slashed open the window screen right next to the radio operator's console with his machete. He tossed the white phosphorus grenade inside, grabbed the second grenade from his belt, jerked out the pin, and dropped it right behind the startled radio operator's chair. Then he spun around, took one quick step away, and dived for the modest protection afforded by the edge of the armory building. Behind him, the black Vietnamese night turned suddenly white.

The first sound Gerber heard following the distinct bang of Smith springing open Jessup's cell was the whoosh of Bocker letting go with the RPG. He yelled at Wilson, who seemed frozen to the side of the building, but to his credit, the CIA man broke loose and moved toward his targets, as he had been briefed to do. Gerber moved without hesitation to the nearest tent, flipped open the door, and flicked the grenade inside. He did the same with the second tent, then jumped sideways and rolled around the corner of the administration building. As soon as the grenades went off, he tossed a third grenade through the open doorway of the generator shack, and dived back around the corner of the admin building. Behind him he could feel the heat coming like a wave from the radio shack and knew that Fetterman had been successful.

Gerber fired three long bursts into the NCO tents, emptying the magazine on his AK-47. He hit the magazine release and knocked the empty mag clear of the weapon, inserted a full one, and ducked back around the corner.

Getting up on one knee, he fired a short burst at the front of the generator shed, then rushed inside. There was no one there. He ducked back out the door and tossed a thermate grenade up against the side of the diesel generator. To his left, the radio shack was already burning fiercely.

Bocker had fired all six rocket-propelled grenades and hit all six barracks before shifting around to the other side of the supply building. He added his firepower to Wilson's and Bao's, raking the tents with his submachine gun. Then he slapped in another magazine, sprinted to the front corner of the supply building, and dropped to one knee. Loading and firing the RPG-7 with machine gun-like precision, he put another six rounds into the barracks, causing extensive damage and setting one of them on fire.

Behind him, Wilson had sunk to one knee, and with trembling hands was fumbling to get a fresh magazine inserted into his AK-47. Bocker thought the man was acting strangely and wondered if he'd been hit, but there was no time to check on him.

Bao slid into place beside Bocker and began to rake the barracks with long bursts from the RPD, pausing only long enough to pick up the first half of the ammunition belt when it fell free of the gun after he had fired fifty rounds. He stuck the metal link-belt through his shoulder harness so he could carry it, and resumed firing.

When the det-cord blew, snapping the padlock shackles with an explosive velocity of 21,000 feet per second, Smith scuttled back over to the pit and yanked open the cage door. He yelled at Jessup to stand up, but the man didn't move. As Smith had feared might happen, the man had either been stunned or temporarily deafened by the explosion. Grabbing the long-handled bolt cutters, he dropped into the pit and switched on his flashlight, flooding the tiny cubicle with red light.

Smith first tried the keys he had been given. To his amazement, they worked, and he quickly removed Jessup's leg irons and handcuffs without recourse to the bolt cutters. When he pulled the blindfold off the major's face, Jessup just stared at him. Dressed in a West German camouflage suit and boots, with his face covered with camouflage grease paint and carrying an AK-47, Smith didn't look much like an American Special Forces sergeant sent to rescue the pilot.

"Are you an American?" shouted Jessup, much louder than necessary.

"U.S. Army Special Forces," said Smith. "Let's go, we don't have much time."

"What?" Jessup yelled again. "I'm sorry! I can't hear anything!"

Smith smiled indulgently and held a finger to his lips to indicate to the other man that he should be quiet. Then he jerked his thumb rapidly upward several times, indicating they should climb out of the pit, and made a stirrup with his hands to boost Jessup up.

When Jessup pulled himself out on the ground and looked around, he wanted to crawl back down in the hole. Although he could hear none of it, he could clearly see the tremendous destruction occurring about him. It looked as though the whole camp was either blowing up or burning down.

Smith pulled himself out of the hole and glanced quickly around. Then he grabbed the AK-47 he had taken from the NVA sentry and shoved both it and the dead man's chest webbing, which contained six spare magazines for the rifle, into Jessup's hands. From the blank expression on the major's face, Smith knew the man had no idea how to fire the weapon. He showed Jessup how to hold the assault rifle and how to take off the safety catch. Then, noticing a small group of men starting toward them across the parade ground, he yelled at them.

"Dos! Dos!"

Although there was considerable noise from explosions across the camp and in the barracks area and the air was filled with the rattle and chatter of AKs and submachine guns, Smith had no doubt the men were close enough to hear him. When they failed to respond to the shouted challenge, he pointed them out to Jessup and picked up his own weapon.

Jessup loosed one long burst from his rifle, emptying the magazine without hitting anyone. Smith flipped the selector on his AK to full auto, the position marked AB in the Cyrillic Russian alphabet, and squeezed off three short bursts, killing all five men.

Smith then motioned for Jessup to get down and keep low while he showed him how to change magazines on his rifle. Jessup made it plain that he wanted to leave the area immediately, but Smith indicated to him that they should wait. Since the Green Beret sergeant seemed to know what he was doing, and since Jessup couldn't tell that he outranked the man because Smith was wearing no insignia, he obeyed.

*   *   *

Across the compound, Bocker had now fired eighteen high-explosive grenades into the barracks, effectively destroying all six buildings and setting three of them ablaze. It appeared that only thirty-five or forty men had succeeded in escaping the destruction caused by the grenade launcher, and except for about two dozen who had crawled away to the north after slipping out the back of one barracks and who seemed to be unarmed, all those who had made it out of the buildings had been quickly cut down by Bao with the RPD.

Gerber had considered that it would be nice to rifle a few of the offices in the administrative building for any interesting papers, although that wasn't part of the mission, but he had too few men and too little time for such a search.

He collected Bocker, Bao, and Wilson and told them to head for the armory and join up with Fetterman and Tyme. Then, as a final thought, he taped an incendiary grenade to the side of the supply building and attached a piece of trip wire to the pin to give himself a head start. When he was about thirty feet away, he yanked on the wire, pulling the pin, and ran after his men.

As Smith watched the flaming barracks from his new position near the maintenance shop, the camp's generator ground to a halt and the lights went out. Although noticeable, it made little difference in the overall illumination. The many fires burning about the compound threw running men rapidly from silhouette into stark relief and back into shadow.

Suddenly a group of twenty-five or thirty men

appeared near the far side of the parade ground, running toward him. Several were armed, and started shooting.

Smith pushed Jessup to the ground, crouched behind the edge of the building, and touched off the front rank of claymores. A torrent of steel pellets tore across the open ground and ripped into bodies, tearing at uniforms, flesh, and equipment with equal abandon and projecting a solid wall of burning gasoline all along the edge of the parade ground. The smell of flaming bodies filled the air.

Across the camp, the two elements of the assault team had reunited.

Gerber deployed his men to provide covering fire as Tyme and Fetterman worked rapidly to rig the armory for demolition. The men secured four demolition blocks, each containing about two and a quarter pounds of plastic explosive, to the lower walls of the building and linked them with det-cord. Fetterman then installed a fifteen-second delay detonator and signaled to Gerber that they were ready to blow the building.

Just at that moment, the team came under heavy fire from the machine gun in the camp's watchtower. Someone had apparently slipped into the structure unobserved during the confusion.

No one was injured by the firing, however, and a final round from Bocker with the RPG-7 brought it to an abrupt stop, vaporizing the top of the tower.

Gerber signaled Fetterman to blow the building, and the master sergeant pulled the pin on the delay detonator. The men then ran through the wrecked officers' quarters and around the mess hall and kitchen before throwing themselves to the ground.

The resultant blast was substantial.

Despite the danger of occasional firing and stray rounds cooking off from the burning armory and other buildings, the men made it across the roadway and open area that separated the mess hall from the motor pool. There they found McMillan waiting for them in a truck, the engine idling.

McMillan immediately leaped from the cab and motioned for Tyme to take the wheel. McMillan ducked around the corner of the shop and yelled, "Let's go!" at Smith. The medical specialist then climbed into the back of the truck, where he would be able to give Jessup a cursory examination once they were clear of the camp.

As Smith scrambled aboard with Jessup, Bao set up the RPD with the bipod of the machine gun resting on the cab of the truck. Gerber climbed into the cab, and the rest climbed on board.

"All present and accounted for, sir!" Fetterman called from the back of the truck.

"Let's get the hell out of here," said Gerber.

Tyme put the truck in gear and let out the clutch.

As they rolled out of the motor pool, McMillan tossed a smoke grenade into a slowly spreading puddle of gasoline. The flammable liquid caught fire at once, sending a stream of fire racing along the parked row of vehicles and enveloping the maintenance garage in a massive conflagration.

The last thing Fetterman saw before they crashed the front gate and roared out onto the road was the

Harley-Davidson. The motorcycle was surrounded by the blaze, burning, burning.

Then the fuel dump exploded.

McMillan gave Jessup a quick examination in the back of the bouncing truck as they raced away from the exploding, burning camp. Except for a few minor lacerations and contusions, the man seemed okay but complained of a dull pain that came and went in his lower back, becoming sharp at times. It was difficult to tell without a proper examination, but McMillan feared the air force officer had compressed a disk in his spine, either upon ejection from the U-2 or by making an improper parachute landing. The described symptoms were consistent with such a diagnosis and, if accurate, could indicate a fairly serious problem. If the disk should become pinched or slip out of alignment, due to vigorous physical activity, the man would require strong analgesics, and possibly muscle relaxants or even a sedative. He would certainly be unable to walk, and being carried over rough terrain on a makeshift litter wouldn't improve his condition. Surgery might even be indicated, then, and McMillan wasn't qualified to perform that sort of procedure.

McMillan gave Jessup a spare set of camouflage fatigues and a pair of tennis shoes to put on. They had been brought along because the Special Forces soldiers had assumed that Jessup's uniform would be taken away from him by the NVA. While the pilot dressed and Fetterman pulled his camo suit on over his night-fighter costume, McMillan held a brief conversation with Gerber through the open rear window of the truck's cab.

"He seems to be in pretty good shape, and his hearing is returning to normal," the medical specialist shouted above the noise of the truck engine and the dwindling explosions in the distance. "Says he got knocked temporarily deaf when Smith blew open the cage door."

"What about the back problem?" Gerber shouted back.

"No way of telling for sure. He might go right along without it ever amounting to much, or he might fold up on us like an accordion. There's no way to tell until it happens. With this kind of injury, usually even X rays aren't much help."

Gerber nodded his understanding. There was nothing they could do but press onward and hope for the best.

Wilson interrupted them. "Captain Gerber," he said, "I'm afraid we have a problem of major proportion."

Gerber wanted to laugh. They had successfully penetrated into North Vietnam, raided an NVA camp, and probably inflicted a hundred casualties, all in violation of international law and opinion, to rescue the pilot of an aircraft sent to spy on the Chinese communists, also in violation of international law and opinion. At any moment now, they would have the entire North Vietnamese army chasing them, and if they were cornered, they would very likely be killed or, if captured, shot as spies, probably after being tortured. If that wasn't enough of a problem of major proportion, Gerber didn't know what was.

"What is it, Mr. Wilson?" he asked tiredly as Tyme braked the truck to a halt and the men prepared to abandon it and move through the dense jungle on foot.

"I've just spoken with Major Jessup, and I'm afraid that it's exactly as we feared."

"What's exactly as who feared, Mr. Wilson? What in the name of Sam Hill are you talking about?"

"The camera. The film. The U-2. Jessup says part of the destruct charges didn't work properly. He's fairly sure the camera may still be intact. He says there was a company of NVA sent out from the camp to look for it, but they haven't found it yet. They only left shortly before we arrived. I'm afraid, Captain, that we're going to have to go after the airplane."

Gerber looked at the man and wanted to tell him to go to hell, but he knew the CIA agent was right. Jessup's rescue would be meaningless if the information on the film in the high-altitude reconnaissance camera aboard the U-2 spy plane were allowed to fall into the hands of the NVA. The North Vietnamese would certainly pass both camera and film on to either their Russian or Chinese allies.

Gerber let out a deep sigh. "Wilson," he said, "you sure know how to make my day."

CHAPTER 8 _____

For ten minutes, while most of the team rested, Gerber crawled through some of the thickest undergrowth he had ever seen, trying to spot signs of a pursuit. He was sure that there had to be one, but whoever they were, they were good. He couldn't hear them and hadn't seen them for nearly two hours.

He worked his way back to the others. Tyme and Fetterman were waiting for him and watching the trail. Wilson and Jessup were sitting, nearly under a large bush, with their eyes closed. Bocker was keeping an eye on them. Smith had gone off somewhere else to plant one of his boobytraps. He had taken Bao with him.

Smith pulled the pin on a grenade and slipped it into an empty can from the C-rations. The can held the safety lever in place. He tied a thick string to the top of the grenade and then hid the can in a bush, anchoring it so that it wouldn't come loose. He

141

stretched the string across the trail so that anyone walking along would yank on the string, pulling the grenade out of the can.

He made sure that Bao understood what he had done and what the results would be. Then, together, they moved back to the others.

When they got there, Gerber said, "Okay, it seems that we've gotten clear. Let's see if we can find the village now."

Without another word, they moved off, in single file. Bao, with his crutch, and Fetterman were near the front, just behind Smith, who now had the point. He had oriented himself with Gerber's old, French map, and thought that he could find his way to the village—provided the village hadn't moved.

After two hours, he stopped to let the others catch up. Again, they examined the map and could find no landmarks. One small stream looked like the next, and there were no villages, hamlets, mountains, or lakes that would provide a precision fix. He looked at the map, around at the tall trees that hid everything behind a wall of green in the triple canopy jungle, and shrugged.

Gerber took the map, turned it twice, and then handed it to Bao. "You have an idea of where the village is?"

"Why don't we just go to the plane?" asked Wilson.

"Fine. Where is it?"

"Major Jessup said that he thought it had gone down about ten miles from where he was captured."

Gerber looked at the air force officer and said, "And where, on this map, do you think that was?"

Feeling somewhat guilty about all that had been

done to secure his release, he took the map and examined it. Although he had expected something different than the flight charts that he was used to, this threw him for a loop. The legend, on the bottom, which was in French, seemed to contain nothing that he recognized. Without a word, he handed it back to Gerber.

"Now," said Gerber. "Let me explain this one last time. We have to find the village because we need their help locating that airplane. Not to mention the fact that we will be able to get a good night's sleep there. The tribesmen will mount the guard, and although we'll have to supplement them, we'll be able to get a good deal of rest."

He turned to Bao. "How far is it?"

"I not know. These people, they might have moved their village because of the communists. But we not have to find it. All we have to do is get close, then they find us. Once close, we will have help."

"You see now, Wilson. This has been thought out. We know what we're doing and could do it a lot better if we didn't have to fight you every step of the way."

"I'm sorry that you feel that way, Captain. I'm only trying to ensure that the mission is completed to the satisfaction of the people in Washington."

For a moment Gerber stared at Wilson. Then he said, "This is not the place to discuss it." He nodded at Tyme, who took the point.

A few minutes later, they were again moving through the jungle. They had veered to the east and then back to the south. At one point, Tyme insisted on climbing a tree, hoping that he could get high enough to spot a clue as to their location, but there was nothing obvious. They had to rely on their last known position, which was the POW camp. They had found it. Now all they had to do was find the Tai village.

Late in the morning, during the heat of the day, they holed up. Gerber and Fetterman kept watch first, followed by Tyme, Smith, McMillan, and Bao. Jessup and Wilson just sat there, stuffing more food in their faces and drinking great quantities of water.

About dusk, just as they were getting ready to move out again, Bao thought he heard something. He pointed toward the sound and Gerber nodded, slipping off the safety of the AK-47. Tyme and Fetterman both picked up their weapons and moved away from the others, taking firing positions. Bocker dropped away, as a rear guard, and Smith stayed where he was to guard Wilson and Jessup, although Jessup still had the AK-47 Smith had taken off the dead NVA soldier.

For five minutes, nothing moved in the jungle. The only noise was from animals and a slight breeze rattling leaves. Gerber raised a questioning eyebrow and then asked Bao if he was sure that he had heard something.

"Yes, Captain Mack. I hear something."

Gerber turned back to watch the jungle, knowing that if the enemy was out there, and knew how to move, he would never see them until it was too late. Then he looked up, and near a large bush that was hugging the base of a giant tree, he saw one man dressed in a loincloth and holding a crossbow.

Then, around them, he saw more of the men. They were slipping through the trees, moving in on the small patrol. Gerber didn't respond. He kept his eyes on the man he had seen first and whispered to Bao, "Are they friendly?"

Bao stood up, favoring his broken leg, held up one hand in a typical Tai greeting, and then said, in the Nung dialect, "I am here with friends to fight the communists."

There was a moment of silence, and then Bao added that they would like to go to the village.

Gerber said, "Tell them that we can give them weapons to help them fight. Weapons that we have taken from the slain enemy."

This time there was a response from the trees. Bao translated. "He say they want all our weapons."

"Tell him no, but if they help us, we'll see that they are able to get some more. Tell him that we'll show them how to fight the communists."

"We not be here that long," protested Bao.

"We'll be here long enough to show them some of the rudiments of small-unit combat."

For several minutes the discussion went on. Finally, the Nung tribesmen agreed to take the Special Forces men to their camp, but only if they were given some weapons before they left. And the Nung leader was careful to warn them that many of his men would be following them at a distance. At the first sign of betrayal, all the Green Berets would be killed.

For most of the night, they climbed upward. The pace was quick, and the natives made no noise. Gerber and his men were able to keep up, although they were sweating heavily. Gerber could feel the strain in his leg muscles and in his back. His mouth was dry from the exertion. He couldn't believe that Bao, whose leg had been broken only a couple of days earlier, who was forced to use a sapling as a crutch, was able to stay with the pace. He didn't complain about pain. Although is face was pale and covered with perspiration, he just kept moving, staying behind the leader of the tribesmen.

Bocker and Smith had taken Wilson's pack and split the load so that the CIA man would be able to keep up. Wilson was told to help Jessup. Tyme and Fetterman were near the end of the column for security, each carrying several weapons, including those captured from the NVA.

Late the next afternoon, after a grueling night, they came to a wooden bridge that had vines for supports and railings. The crosspieces were lashed together with more vines. It didn't look like it would support much weight.

On the far side, there wasn't anything to be seen. The jungle had closed in on the trail, but Gerber knew that the village had to be close.

One by one they crossed the bridge. It shook under the weight of the Americans, and dirt and moss dropped off the bottom as they walked across, but it held.

Ten minutes later they were on the outskirts of a village of shabby hootches set on stilts. The sides of most were woven from bamboo and palm leaves. The roofs were made the same way, with a second layer of palm situated crossways. Notched logs were leaned against the hootches to provide steps into them. A couple of dogs ran loose, but there was no evidence of anyone living there, other than a couple of unattended cooking fires burning near the center of the village.

Off to the right came the smell of human excrement. Garbage was piled to one side of a long hootch. There were a couple of large puddles of standing water that gave off a stench.

The tribesmen ran ahead into the village, ignoring for a moment the men they had brought with them. Gerber pointed right and left, and Tyme and Smith moved quickly to provide some security. Bao walked ahead slowly, almost as if waiting for an invitation. Wilson and Jessup collapsed to the ground, happy for a chance to rest, not caring about the odor.

Gerber and Fetterman waited, standing where the Tais had left them, watching. Slowly, people began appearing from the trees. First there were only more men, all armed with crossbows or knives, and then women, and finally the children. They didn't rush forward but advanced slowly, as if afraid of the strangers.

Bao had gotten to the center of the village, near the long house. He reached out to support himself against the wall and waited.

The head man spoke briefly, waving at the people, trying to herd them toward the long house. He stepped up on the lower notch of the log ladder leading into the long house and began a speech, occasionally pointing toward Gerber and his party. He motioned Bao forward, introduced him, and let him speak.

At a sign from Bao, the Green Berets, Wilson, and Jessup, came forward. The villagers kept their distance at first, studying the newcomers. Some of the children mingled with the strangers, surprised by their height and size.

With the speech-making finished, the head man ushered the newcomers into the long house. At the far end was a young woman trying to light a fire. The wood was piled on a large, flat stone that was against the far wall. Over it was a hole in the roof that was supposed to draw the smoke out. It was only partially effective.

Fetterman walked along one wall, touching the thatching once in a while. He stopped at the fire, moved around it, and looked out the door at that end. He finished the circuit and said to Gerber, "Not very defensible."

"Don't worry about it. We'll take care of that later."

"Captain, we're sitting in the middle of this village with no security around us. I don't like it."

Gerber smiled and nodded at the chief. To Fetterman he said, "We'll get someone out in a couple of minutes. Right now, the important thing is to not offend these people. They can help make our mission a success, or they can sneak in here at night and cut our throats."

Wilson stepped closer and said, "How long are we going to stay here?"

"As long as it takes."

Bao said, "We have food here soon."

"I'm not eating anything these people bring," said Wilson.

Gerber looked Wilson in the eyes. "You will do nothing to offend these people. You will eat the food they bring. You don't have to eat much, but you will eat some. These people could become real allies, could ensure that we succeed, but not if you do something stupid. If you offend them, they'll probably try to kill you. And the way you've been pissing and moaning since we started this mission, Wilson, I just might let them. You've been nothing but baggage."

For a moment Wilson held his gaze, and then dropped his eyes. He said, "All right, Captain, but don't think this is the end. We'll talk about this later."

"When we're in Saigon, sipping beers, surrounded by a couple of U.S. Army divisions, I'll be glad to talk about it."

Bao, seeing that Gerber and Wilson had finished their hostile exchange, moved close to the captain. "Chief want know how he may serve you. He want you happy in his village."

"You tell him that it is our honor to be here." Gerber looked at Fetterman. "Tony, you want to bring a couple of those AKs over here."

When he got them, he handed three of them to Bao. "You give these to the chief. Make sure that he knows how to use them, though I have little doubt that he already does. Tell him it's only part of the ones we'll provide for him."

Before he could say more, nine women, each carrying a pot of food, entered. They walked slowly to the center of the long house and knelt, setting the pots on a woven bamboo mat.

The women wore little. They had a cloth around their waists and sandals on dirty feet. They all had long, black hair that looked as if it had been recently combed. Not one of them looked to be older than twenty.

The chief followed them in and stood near them. He beckoned the Americans forward. Bao went with them. He watched the chief, and when the chief sat, Bao did the same, waving to the others. The women then began serving them from the various pots, placing the food on pieces of palm leaf.

When everyone had a portion, the chief lifted the palm leaf nearly to his chin and, using his fingers, pushed the food at his mouth.

Fetterman did the same, chewing rapidly and almost swallowing a chunk of meat whole. "Guards, Captain?"

"Be patient. We'll get someone out there in a couple of minutes."

McMillan sniffed the food and then took a large bite. He chewed it slowly, as if savoring the flavor. To Bao, he said, "What is this stuff?"

Bao looked at the palm leaf and said, "You have dog. There is monkey in one pot, snake in another, and deer in another."

Wilson suddenly looked as if he was about to be sick. Fetterman grinned at him and took an extra large bite. Tyme saw this and did the same. Gerber smiled and said cheerily, "Eat up, Mr. Wilson, or you might find yourself dead in a stew."

After a few minutes, Gerber said, "Lieutenant Bao, would you tell the chief that as a precaution, I would like Sergeants Bocker and Tyme to back-track our trail a ways to make sure the communists haven't been following us."

Bao translated the message and waited while the

chief replied with a long speech. Bao said, "Chief say that no communists follow. He leave men behind to watch. They out there now."

"Then tell him we appreciate his effort on our behalf, but we would like to repay his kindness by having some of our men help with those duties."

Again Bao spoke, listened, and then said, "Chief say that he would be honored to have such great warriors, who kill Cong and bring their weapons as gifts, help."

Gerber turned to Tyme. "Okay, grab your weapons and go. Take Bocker with you. Stay out about four hours. When you get back, Fetterman and Smith can go."

"How about me?" said McMillan.

"I think we might better use you on sick call. Treat some of the disease around here. Another way of repaying the hospitality."

Tyme and Bocker disappeared out the door. They saw a couple of villagers, who ignored them. Tyme wanted to circle the village to see if there were any obvious routes of attack. He found that the best way would be to come across the bridge, but the enemy could come up the side of the mountain if they wanted. A steep, hazardous climb, but not completely impossible.

From there, he took Bocker and entered the jungle, figuring that a roving patrol about a klick out would be the best. Move slowly, and listen for the enemy.

In the long house, the dinner party moved into its second phase. The women picked up the pots, palm leaves, and the remains of the meal and took them outside. Then, one by one, they came back in, moving toward the Americans. Gerber looked at Bao to ask about this.

"Women are here to please you. Anything you want. For all the night."

Ignoring everything else, Wilson said, "Shouldn't we start searching for the plane? We can't waste time here."

Gerber looked from Bao to Wilson and back to Bao, but said to Wilson, "Where do we search? Exactly where are we now? The only way to find it is with the help of these people. I already told you that."

One of the women moved behind Gerber and began rubbing his shoulders. The others were doing the same to the rest of the team. Gerber said to Bao, "What's happening?"

"Women here as hospitality. Nung share with us. This very great honor."

"Time is wasting," repeated Wilson.

"Look, Wilson," said Gerber, stepping away from the woman who was trying to massage him, "these people know the area. We tell them what we want and let them find it and guide us to it. It's about the only way we're going to find the plane. Jessup is no help because he was busy bailing out. All he knows is that it came down somewhere around here. We'd never find it alone."

The woman moved around to Gerber's front and began unbuttoning his fatigue shirt. He grabbed her hands and tried to smile at her.

"You think a bunch of ignorant savages will be able to help us with that?" said Wilson.

"Bao, tell them to wait a minute. Give me a chance to think."

Bao began a rapid-fire exchange with the chief.

"Wilson, just shut up right now, okay? Bao and the chief will discuss the problem. Then Jessup and I and Fetterman will go over the maps and see if we can limit the search area. These people know everything that happens around here, and if the plane is down, they'll know where or be able to find it. Now leave me alone."

"Chief say women are ours. Say that only way we be completely trusted is if we have women. Say that it is a sign of respect for great warriors to have women. We not able to say no."

"Oh, Christ," said Gerber, "That's all we need."

The woman moved back to Gerber and began working on the buttons again.

"Wait a minute," he said. "Just wait a minute."

Everything stopped. All the people looked at Gerber because he had spoken so harshly.

Gerber felt it building up on him. Everyone standing there talking to him from every different angle. He wanted a second to organize his thoughts, but no one was giving it to him. This wasn't battle, so he had time to think, to organize, and he could see no reason why he should be under this pressure. No reason whatsoever.

He turned to Bao and said, "Let's get everyone to sit down for a moment. Then we'll talk to the chief."

Jessup had eased himself into a corner, almost as if to gain a little privacy. He had his shirt off and was holding on to the Tai woman gingerly as he kissed her neck.

The women all sat down, outside the circle of men, and waited for something to be decided.

Gerber's mind raced ahead. This was a complication that he didn't need. The women were the best that the Nungs had to offer, and to refuse would be a great insult. It could cause the tribesmen to attack the Americans. They might even turn them over to the communists. They certainly wouldn't continue to help. The women were now a symbol of the trust and the affection between the Nungs and the Americans. It was a situation that demanded quick thinking and diplomacy.

"Please tell the chief that his hospitality is without comparison in the world. He makes his guests feel as if they have finally returned home."

As Bao translated, the chief sat smiling and nodding. He said something in reply.

"Chief say they welcome those who help them kill communists. The communists harass them, kill them, and steal the food of the Nung people. Steal women too. Chief happy to have us here."

They had now reached the point where Gerber had to refuse the women without offending the people. He wasn't sure that it could be done. He just knew that he had to try. It grated on him. He just couldn't use women that way.

To Bao, he said, "Please tell the chief that in my country, it is considered a big insult to women for a man to be with them too soon after battle. Tell the chief that we believe that great harm will come to the women and cause the men much bad luck in future battles."

Bao sat there, not speaking. Smoke from the fire swirled around them. Everyone was quiet, waiting.

Bao said, "I cannot say that. It not true. I no lie to chief. I no thief. I no liar."

Gerber rubbed his head just above his right eyebrow. Quietly, he said, "Sometimes it is necessary to lie. Sometimes, to spare the feelings of another, one must lie. We call it a white lie because it is meant to do good."

"I not lie to chief."

"Suppose," said Gerber, "that you bought a shirt that you thought was beautiful. You show it to me, and I think it is the worst thing I have ever seen. Should I tell you that, or should I say that I like it? Should I hurt your feelings over it?"

Bao didn't say anything.

"You see the point, don't you? I tell you I like it and no one is hurt by it?"

For a moment Bao was quiet, digesting the information. In the last few days he had learned that it was all right to steal, as long as it was for a good cause. Now he was learning that it was all right to lie, as long as the intentions were for the best. It made no sense to him because he had believed that lying and stealing were wrong. There were no areas of gray, only black and white.

Bao was getting a quick education in the ways of Western civilization. There were many levels to operate on, some of them so subtle as to be nearly non-existent. You could lie, if the lie was not meant to harm. You could steal, if you were recovering your own property. Yet Bao knew that the Green Berets were men of honor. Men who would not betray his trust.

He had trusted Lieutenant Johnny, and Lieutenant

Johnny told him to trust Gerber. Both were men of honor. He wasn't sure that he understood the difference in the lies, but to Gerber it had seemed perfectly clear.

From the other side of the room, Jessup said, "I don't mind, Captain. If it will help the mission, I will gladly bed one of the ladies." He knew that his father couldn't object to this because it was necessary for the mission. Besides, his father had figuratively screwed hundreds for advancement. He was doing it literally.

"You keep your mouth shut, Jessup," said Gerber, ignoring his rank. "If we need something from you, we'll ask."

Gerber tried another track.

"Bao, you know the men are very tired. We have done much fighting and been marching almost continuously since we raided the NVA camp. Tomorrow we must begin looking for the airplane. The men need rest more than they need women. Surely you can see the logic in that. Yet we are greatly honored by the chief's offer and have no wish to offend him by refusing such honor."

Bao could understand that, but still seemed reluctant.

Suddenly Fetterman had an inspiration. He leaned forward between the two men. "Bao, you trust me, don't you? You know that I'm your friend."

"Bao jump from plane with Sergeant Tony. I trust you. You show me how to fly without airplane, using big umbrella. You are friend."

"Well, Bao, you know that I am a family man. You've heard me speak of Mrs. Fetterman and the kids. My people have a strong sense of family, as do

the Tai people. Among my people, it is considered
wrong for a man with a family to sleep with a woman
who is not his wife. This is also true for the Tai, is it
not?''

Bao nodded. ''Usually true, but sometimes there
are exceptions. By offering women, chief is offering
wives. That make Americans members of chief's
tribe. Great honor. Sergeant Tony understand these
not Saigon prostitutes. These honorable women. Two
of them are daughters of chief.''

''Oh, shit,'' said Jessup. ''I didn't realize he was
trying to marry us to his daughters. Father wouldn't
like that at all.''

Fetterman glared at him, then went on.

''That is exactly why we can't accept. I've already
got a wife. In American culture, it is not possible for
a man to have more than one wife. To do so is a terrible
insult to his first wife and to all her tribe. For this
reason, I cannot accept the chief's offer, although I
am greatly honored by it. Captain Gerber and the
others are not married, but because they honor my
beliefs, they will not ask me to violate them. Also,
because they are my friends, they do not wish to be
with women while I cannot. Besides, we must leave
this place tomorrow, and it may be a long time
before we can come back. It would not be right for
them to take wives when they will not be here to hunt
for them and provide them with a home and family.''

Bao nodded and said, ''I tell chief.''

''But be careful,'' said Gerber. ''We want him to
understand that we mean no offense, but it is our
custom.''

When Bao finished, there was a sharp bark from

the chief and the women got up to leave. The chief stood, smiling down at Gerber. He made a long speech.

Bao translated. "Chief say that he learn that other peoples have many strange beliefs. He say that he will not force anyone to go against his own belief. He understand. When this is over, he ask that you come back again. Then they have a full feast, beat water buffalo to death, and drink all night. Then you sleep with women in honor of Nung beliefs."

Gerber returned the chief's smile and said, "Tell him we would be honored. We may not be able to return immediately, but we will remember the chief's kindness."

The chief walked to the door and stopped. He turned and said something.

"Chief say that he will send women back tomorrow with breakfast. He hope we have a good night, but think we will be cold without women to keep us warm."

It had been dark for an hour when Bocker returned. He nearly ran through the village and leaped into the long house. He saw Gerber had broken down an AK-47 and was cleaning it. He walked over to him and said, "I think we've located a platoon of NVA near here."

Gerber looked up from his weapon and said, "Go on."

"About a klick out we spotted the point of an NVA unit. We waited and counted thirty-seven of them, moving more or less in this direction, but moving slowly. We might have fifteen minutes before they arrive."

"Where's Tyme?"

"At the bridge. We don't think they'll be able to climb the back side of the mountain, and if they try, it'll take them three, four hours."

"Okay." Gerber turned to the others, who were now all listening. "Smith, take the RPD and get out to the bridge with Tyme. The rest of us will meet you there. Bao, tell the chief that we think that the communists are close. We're going out to meet them."

Jessup said, "What about us?"

"We'll all go. Keep the party together so that we don't have to double back. I want to lead the communists away from here to protect these people."

Bao returned with the chief. Bao said, "Chief say that his men want chance to kill communists. They go with us."

Gerber knew that there was no way that he could refuse the chief's offer this time. Even if he told the chief that his men couldn't go, they would anyway. All he could do was try to set it up so that the fewest possible got hurt, and so that they stayed out of the way.

"Tell the chief to have his men here quickly and we will deploy. Try to convince him that his men should stay on this side of the bridge. Tell them that we'll be on the other side and try to force the communists toward them."

At the bridge, Gerber hesitated only long enough to give some instructions to the Tais. He asked them to stay put so that they would be able to ambush the communists. He didn't really expect them to stay, especially when they heard the shooting, but there was always a chance they might.

Fetterman rushed across the bridge and headed down the trail, leading the rest of the team. He found Tyme and Smith coming back toward them. They held a whispered conference and then moved into the trees along the trail, setting up an ambush there. Fetterman made sure that both Jessup and Wilson had weapons, but put them near the center of the ambush and cautioned them not to fire until he did.

In a couple of minutes, Gerber joined them. Far down the trail they heard the NVA. They weren't making much noise, just enough to be heard. Still, the idea that they were in their own country and didn't have to worry about enemy action was with them. They weren't as careful as they should have been.

Gerber was on the ground, near a large tree, where he could see down the trail. He saw the point man almost before he was ready for him. He whispered the observation to Fetterman so that the American patrol could be alerted.

The point man walked right by without looking either right or left. He hurried on, as if he knew the destination, which was apparently the village.

The main body came up then. Gerber pulled out a grenade, got rid of the pin, and tossed the bomb. The explosion shattered the night. At that moment, everyone else opened fire, and a dozen of the enemy fell on the trail. The others broke in all directions, fleeing.

Several of them found cover on the other side of the trail and began shooting back. The bullets cut through the trees and bushes over the Green Berets' heads. Broken twigs, torn leaves, and pieces of bark rained down on them. The volume of firing increased until it was nearly a continuous roar.

Tyme and Smith crawled away from the trail, turned, and then paralleled it for fifty feet until they were clear of the firefight. Together, they leaped up, jumped the trail, and fell among the bushes and trees filled with the NVA. They opened fire from the new position.

Part of the enemy had broken toward the village when the shooting began. They ran up the trail, ignoring everything, until they came to the bridge. Two of them started across as the Tais there opened fire. The two on the bridge fell, riddled with bullets from the captured weapons that Gerber had given the tribesmen.

The NVA there engaged the Tais, neither side inflicting any more casualties. Neither side could advance because of the deep ravine and the narrow bridge.

Wilson crouched behind the Special Forces' line, his back to a large tree. He heard the bullets whistling through the air near him and even felt the impact of some of them in the trunk of the tree. He wanted to shoot, to run, to get down, but couldn't move. He had never experienced anything like this. It was the first real firefight he had been in.

It wasn't the first shoot-out. He had been in several on missions with the Agency. But most of them had lasted less than ten seconds. Only one of them had lasted for a full minute, and had involved only three people. There was a limited amount of ammunition. But nothing like this.

Nothing like fifty or sixty men, firing hundreds of rounds for over ten minutes. He could hear shouting from the NVA and some from the Green Berets. They were using grenades. There were shouts from the wounded and the dying.

In his other gun battles, he knew that if he had been wounded, there would be hospitalization and doctors nearby. Here there was only McMillan, a medic.

This wasn't an urban environment either. Wilson knew how to maneuver in the streets for the best advantage. But the jungle was an unknown. And if he wasn't killed by the bullets and shrapnel, he could be killed by a snake, or even a venomous insect.

Suddenly he had nothing but respect for Gerber and his men. They were the true professionals here and should be allowed to complete the mission with no further interference from him. He would allow Gerber to do what had to be done so long as it coincided with his mission, and if he survived the next few minutes, he would recommend that Gerber and his men receive some sort of award.

Gerber was aware that the shooting was tapering off. It meant that the NVA were trying to break contact, which was the last thing he wanted them to do. With Fetterman, he crawled to the edge of the trail without shooting. There, they tossed a couple more grenades into the midst of the NVA.

Using the explosions as cover, Fetterman crossed the trail and dived among the enemy. He shot three of them at point-blank range as they tried to flee. A fourth he clubbed and a fifth he bayoneted.

Gerber followed, moving wide to the right. He stepped between two of the enemy, who both turned to fire. Gerber dropped to his knees, and the two NVA soldiers shot each other. Gerber made sure they were dead and moved deeper into the trees.

Tyme and Smith also advanced. Tyme shot an NVA soldier who jumped up in front of him. Smith used his machine gun butt on another. Suddenly, all the shooting around them stopped. Tyme and Smith swept forward, checking the bodies and picking up the weapons.

From the village, they heard a wild burst of firing. Gerber turned to look, but the thick jungle and the darkness prevented him from seeing anything. He tapped Fetterman on the shoulder so that he would come with him. Bocker and McMillan also followed, staying away from the trail.

Cautiously, they crawled toward the bridge until they could see the backs of the NVA soldiers there. They spread out on line and then, on signal from Gerber, opened fire.

The NVA, caught completely by surprise, jumped up and rushed the bridge, but the Tais were ready and cut them down. One NVA threw down his rifle and raised his hands but was killed by a stray bullet. Another jumped into the ravine, screaming until he hit bottom several hundred feet below.

Now the firing was only an occasional shot as two members of the opposing sides stumbled on each other in the dark. Gerber and Fetterman moved back, away from the bridge, so that they could finish checking the ambush site. With Tyme and Smith, they picked up all the weapons and ammunition they could carry.

Wilson showed up then, loaded down with more of the enemy's AKs, and was told to take them to the bridge. The shooting there had stopped, and Bocker had been able to signal the villagers, with the help of Bao, that they were coming back.

The chief, and two of his elders, crossed the bridge and began picking up the remaining weapons, ammunition, and equipment. Bocker helped them.

Gerber gave McMillan a load of weapons and sent him into the village to help anyone who had been wounded. As soon as they had pulled all the dead into the jungle so that they weren't easy to see from the trail, counted the bodies, and picked up the weapons, Gerber and his men went back to the village.

There were twenty-nine dead NVA along the trail near the bridge and lying in the ravine. That meant that some of them had gotten away. It meant that they were compromised at the village and would have to move out rapidly. But he still had time to enlist the aid of the villagers in finding the U-2. At first light, they would start the search.

Gerber had his men pile the weapons and equipment taken from the dead near the long house. He then called the chief over and said, with Bao translating, "Please, take these, all of these weapons and give them to your men. They are fierce warriors. In some small way, I hope that these weapons may repay your kindness and your help."

The chief nodded, smiling so wide that the gaps between his teeth were prominent, even in the poor light, and pawed through the pile. He picked out the best weapon, held it over his head, and then told his men to grab what they wanted. In seconds, the ground was bare.

Gerber grouped his men around him and said, "Smith. Bocker. I want you two to mount the roving patrol until midnight. Then McMillan and I will take over. Everyone plan on moving out about dawn tomorrow. Bao, come with me. We've got to talk with the chief. We're going to need his help at first light, and I don't think he's going to want to stay here very long. Sometime tomorrow those NVA who got away are going to be back, and I have a hunch they're going to be bringing a bunch of their friends we don't want to meet."

CHAPTER 9 _____

THE TAI VILLAGE
IN JUNGLES OF NORTH VIETNAM

The last of the roving patrols, headed by Gerber, entered the village just as the sun was peeking through the thick overcast. Fetterman and Tyme were waiting outside the long house and were nearly surrounded by the Tais. Tyme was eating from a can containing a combat meal. Fetterman was watching the Tais.

"Where are the others?" Gerber asked Fetterman.

"Inside asleep."

Gerber set his weapon down against the side of the long house and let his pack fall to the ground for a moment. He looked at Tyme and said, "Let's all get some food. Justin, why don't you wake the others. We'll move out in about fifteen minutes."

Bao limped to the doorway, rubbing an eye.

"Could you ask the chief to join us over here?" Gerber asked him. "We're going to need him."

While Gerber was eating, the chief appeared, wearing the remnants of a fatigue uniform left by the French a decade earlier. He saw Gerber sitting on the ground outside the long house and squatted near him.

Gerber put his combat meal can aside, swallowed, and got out his map. He spread it out and waited until Bao was near. With Bao's help, Gerber showed the chief where the village was on the map, as near as he could estimate, and then explained what they were looking for. Using the map, he told him where he thought the plane might have crashed. He also explained it in terms of distance and direction so that the Nung chief understood. Then he said that it was very important that the plane be found.

The chief, hearing how large the plane was, thought that it would be only a couple of hours before his men found it. He said if he traded some of the weapons to other villages, he might be able to get their help, and the task would become easier.

Gerber responded that he thought there would be more opportunities to find weapons. Now, he and his men would leave the village because he was afraid that more communists would be coming, and he didn't want to endanger the villagers. He thanked the chief for his help.

The chief expressed his pleasure at the honor of having fought the NVA alongside such fine warriors as the Green Berets and said that the entire village would be moving soon to avoid NVA reprisals.

Fifteen minutes later, with three guides provided by the chief, Gerber and his men crossed the bridge and entered the jungle again. They turned to the southeast, following a well-used trail for a few minutes, and then left it. All around them were the villagers, looking for the downed airplane.

*   *   *

The whole day was spent wandering through the jungle, staying away from most of the trails. Twice they found other groups of tribesmen who were now out searching for the large, black object that had fallen from the sky.

Jessup was no help in the search. He kept saying that if he could get airborne, he could orient himself and tell them where the plane was. Using the old French maps, he could only guess. The landmarks the French infantry used were different from those needed by air force pilots. And over twenty years, the jungle had changed them. All he could say was that he thought that the plane was down about twenty klicks north of the DMZ, but he didn't know for sure.

At noon, they stopped to eat. The guides offered Gerber and his men some of their rice, but Gerber insisted that they try the combat meals.

After a brief rest, they started out again. The pace was not as rapid, but all the Americans were soon sweating heavily. They were drinking their water faster than planned. Suddenly water was becoming a critical item. Then, about four, they crossed a clear stream, and while the Tais drank from it, the Americans filled their canteens, using iodine pills to purify the water.

At dusk, they halted again. Gerber was afraid that a fire would give away their position and said that they would eat their meal cold. He then directed Smith and McMillan to take the first watch while the others caught up on their sleep.

The night passed quietly, except for the prowling

of the animals. Wilson sat beside a tree, claiming that he wasn't tired. And he thought that someone in the camp should be awake, even if there were two men in the jungle watching.

The Tais laughed at the antics of the Americans. When it was dark, the three of them lay down together, using each other's bodies to keep warm. They slept through the whole night without waking. At dawn they woke, ate some rice and raw snake, and waited for the Americans to open their food in metal eggs.

That day was a repeat of the first. They walked through the jungle, avoiding the main trails and paths. They avoided the villages because Gerber said that he didn't want hundreds of people to know they were around. Once or twice, the Tai guides went into a village, searching for information about the airplane, but each time they came back without having discovered anything.

They camped that night, continued with the roving patrols, and tried to sleep. Wilson sat next to a tree again that night, dozing periodically. Jessup didn't sleep at all.

It was midmorning the next day, and Gerber was afraid that they would have to call off the search. They had already overstayed the timeframe of the mission by two days. Originally they had planned only to try to rescue Jessup and then get out. Wilson had changed that with his demand that they find the plane, but they couldn't be running around the jungles of North Vietnam forever. There had to be an alert out for them by now, and it was only a matter of time before the NVA found them, with a force large enough to wipe them out.

They had halted for a rest break when two of the Tais from one of the other search parties slipped up on them. They conferred with the guides for a couple of minutes. One of them turned to Bao and spoke to him rapidly.

Bao said, "Was this thing you look for long and black?"

"You know it was," said Gerber.

"Yes," said Bao. "I was asking question that was asked of me. I think they have found the plane."

"How far?" asked Wilson.

Bao looked at Wilson but turned toward Gerber. Gerber said, "How far?"

The question was asked of the new men and translated for Gerber.

"Four, maybe five hours."

Gerber looked at his watch. "If we move out now, we can get there with a couple of hours of daylight left. Give us a chance to scope out the situation before we have to move in." He turned back to Bao. "Will they lead us to the plane?"

"They say they will, if we give them weapons. They want four of the AK-47s."

Gerber smiled. "You tell them that when we get there, if it is the plane, we will see that each of them gets a weapon with ammunition. Two AKs. Not four."

"Captain," Fetterman cautioned, "we don't have any weapons to spare."

"I know that, but I think we'll have the opportunity to capture a couple in the next few days. Besides, we've still got the Swedish Ks and the RPD."

"You're taking a real chance, Captain."

"No, not really." He gestured at the others. "Let's saddle up and get out of here."

•

They moved through the afternoon jungle without taking a break. It looked to Gerber as if they were walking in circles for the first hour. He checked his compass a number of times and tried to orient himself on the map. Finally he stopped the guides and asked them about it. He was told that there was a large ravine that they had to avoid.

As a precaution, Gerber left Fetterman and Tyme behind to guard the trail. They were to wait for twenty minutes to see if anyone was following. If not, they could catch up.

Less than an hour later, the Tai tribesmen stopped. They pointed to the south and told Bao that the airplane was very close. Gerber told everyone to wait while he and Bocker took a look.

Carefully, they crawled forward, wondering if they would find the U-2. Overhead, Gerber noticed that the tops of a number of trees had been sheared, as if clipped by a low-flying airplane. There were split branches and damage to some of the shorter trees in front of him. It certainly looked just like a plane had plunged through the lush vegetation.

Gerber moved to the right and continued to crawl. He moved around a bush and looked into a small, oblong-shaped clearing. Lying in the middle of it was the fuselage of the U-2. The wings had been snapped from the body. The crumpled remains of one of them was right in front of him. The tail section was jammed up under a couple of the trees, looking as if the plane had hit the ground and spun around.

Off to the side, he saw Bocker. He held a thumb up, telling him that this was it, and then motioned him back. Together, they headed to the point where they had left the others. Fetterman and Tyme had arrived.

Gerber got his people together and told them, "Since it's close to dark now and we won't be able to accomplish anything until morning, I think we should set up an ambush close to the plane. If anyone shows up, we'll be in a good position to defend."

"With the battery lantern I have," said Wilson, "I can get that film package out."

"We can't use the light at night. It would be like a beacon for the NVA. Besides, we'll be here to prevent anyone from taking anything."

"Then everything is there?"

Gerber looked at Wilson. "I don't know for sure. We just made sure that we had found the plane. We didn't approach it."

Wilson was going to protest and then remembered his thoughts during the firefight. This was Gerber's environment, not his. If Gerber thought it best to wait even though he, Wilson, had just voiced his objections, then he would wait. Let Gerber run the show completely. For now.

Before it was pitch dark, they moved into position. Gerber set his men so that they were at the ends of both sides of the ambush. The Tais were near the middle. Jessup and Wilson were immediately behind them, more or less out of the line of fire.

With that ready, everyone ate a quick, cold meal. Gerber then told every other man to sleep for a while. They would rotate the guard until two, when everyone would stay awake. He wasn't sure that it was necessary. They were in North Vietnam, where the NVA and VC could move with impunity day or night. Unless the communists were in a hurry to get somewhere, the enemy might camp until daybreak. On the other hand, if they were on the trail of the Green Berets, they might well push on through the night. Still, it never hurt to be alert, and if things went well, they would be on the SWIFT boats in less than thirty-six hours.

The next morning, they spent two hours watching the airplane, but there was nothing to indicate that it was being watched by anyone else. After a cold breakfast, Gerber posted Tyme and McMillan for security as the rest of them advanced on the downed aircraft. Before he would let either Wilson or Jessup close to it, he had Smith check it for boobytraps. Apparently the NVA had not found it.

Wilson, on the signal from Gerber, came forward. He looked into the cockpit and then at the equipment packages hidden along the fuselage. Other than damage sustained during the crash, they were intact. Either Jessup had not been able to blow them or the charges had failed.

Wilson turned an accusing eye on Jessup.

"I threw the switches," the pilot said. "Then I bailed out. They must not have worked. I told you I couldn't be sure."

In the cockpit, Wilson could see that some of the

switches had been thrown. One or two were still in the "safe" position. "No harm done," said Wilson.

Gerber turned and looked at him. He couldn't believe that Wilson was not jumping all over Jessup for failing to destroy the equipment.

"Give me a screwdriver out of that bag and I'll get the film pod out," said Wilson.

"It's boobytrapped in," said Jessup.

"I know that," countered Wilson. "I also know how to deactivate them."

"Get on with it," said Gerber. "The longer we stay here, the better the chance that someone will find us."

Wilson nodded and crawled under the fuselage. He pushed the buttons that would open the access panel for the camera but found it jammed. He pushed the screwdriver under the edge of the access panel, twisted it, and jammed the screwdriver in deeper. With the heel of his hand, he hit the top of the screwdriver. The panel popped open, nearly striking him in the head.

With that open, he got to his knees and the upper half of his body disappeared into the access well. He shouted, "Give me the pliers, and the Phillips screwdriver."

There was a banging, and then Wilson said, "Jessup, would you give me a hand here."

There was an awkward moment, as Jessup tried to stand up in the hatch. He moved around and, with one arm dangling at his side, had one hand available.

"Hold this," said Wilson, handing him a length of wire. "Keep it taut for a moment, and when I tell you, jerk on it. You need to pull it loose."

Wilson dropped his screwdriver and used the pliers to cut a couple of wires. "Now," he said.

As he had been told, Jessup jerked on the wire and banged his elbow on the edge of the hatch. "Shit!"

"Hold it down," snapped Gerber. "We're still in North Vietnam."

"Okay," said Wilson, "now get down, under here, and I'll drop the film pod to you."

Jessup dropped to his knees and eased his way to the left, so that he could reach up under the fuselage. He saw the bottom of the film pod appear and braced his hands against it so that it wouldn't fall.

"Hold it there a moment," said Wilson.

"I've got it."

Wilson clipped a final wire and said, "Okay, that's it. Let it down."

Jessup dropped it to the ground with a loud thud.

"I said let it down, not drop it."

"Sorry."

Wilson got down and looked over the pod. He saw that part of the film had jammed unexposed. He cranked it around until all the film was housed in the receiver and then used a screwdriver to remove that portion of the package from the pod. That done, he said, "I've got the film."

Jessup watched this and then went back to the cockpit. He found his charts, marked with his flight routes and the areas that he was to photograph. He pulled them out, plus a classified sheet that gave his EEIs, and stuffed both into a pocket of his fatigues.

Wilson joined him. "Anything else that we're going to need?"

"Like what?"

"I don't know. I was just told to get the film pod if I could. I thought maybe there was something else on the aircraft that I hadn't been warned about."

"The only thing I can think of is to destroy the plane."

"The charges didn't work last time."

"Maybe Gerber has something he can do." Jessup walked over to the trees, just like he was in a park, not in North Vietnam surrounded by NVA soldiers.

To Gerber he said, "We're ready to go, but we want to destroy the aircraft. The explosive charges already planted there don't seem to work."

Gerber reached up, grabbed Jessup by the shoulder, and jerked him down, behind the bush. "Would you try to remember where we are. Now, you wait here, and I'll check with Sully Smith."

"You think he can help?"

"If you want it blown up, he can help. If there are explosives on the aircraft, he can use those. If not, he'll think of something."

Sully Smith crawled away from the tree where he had been hidden and, in a crouch, ran to the aircraft. First, he looked into the cockpit to see if there was a broken circuit between the switches and the explosives. He traced a couple of wires but found nothing to indicate why they failed.

Next, he checked the explosives, thinking that there might be something wrong at that end, but all the wires were attached and all the detonators were in place.

"Say, Major," he asked, "where's the battery in this thing?"

Jessup, who had been sitting on the ground under

part of the fuselage, got up and opened an access panel. "Over here."

Smith looked inside and saw that the connection for the battery was tight, but then noticed that a liquid had pooled under it. "There's your problem. No electricity."

While Smith tried to rig up a firing curcuit for the explosives and find out if there was any fuel left in the ruptured tanks, Bao crawled over to Gerber. Leaning close to his ear, Bao said, "Guide say that they hear someone in the jungle. Come this way."

"They know who it is?"

"They say they think it is the communists, but they not sure."

"Get back to your post. If you see or hear anything else, let me know. I'll warn the others."

Gerber crawled around, telling each of his men that someone was coming their way. Then he moved to the plane, told Jessup and Wilson to find some cover. To Smith, he asked, "How long will it take you?"

"Not long, Captain. But I wanted to stay to make sure that it all went up. This is going to be such a makeshift deal that I'm not sure how well the fuselage will burn."

"Make it snappy."

Bao was waiting as he crawled back to his position. He told Gerber, "There are fifteen, maybe twenty NVA coming now."

"You tell the others not to shoot until I do. You will have to make sure that they don't shoot first. We don't want to tip our hand early."

"I do my best, Captain Mack."

Gerber watched Bao head back toward the Nung tribesmen. He knew that he was in the same position that he had been in during the ambush at the village. He had to rely on people he hadn't trained to do something that they didn't believe. From working with the strikers at his own camp, Gerber knew that most of the tribesmen believed that the best way to kill communists was just to kill communists. They couldn't understand some of the more subtle points of ambushes. He hoped Bao could hold them in check.

As Gerber watched the woods, Smith crawled up. He said, "I have it ready, sir. Lined the underside of the fuselage with the jet fuel I salvaged from one of the wing tanks. I put a smoke grenade at the head of the line, so that, when I pull the pin, the flame from the bottom will ignite the fuel. I also set it up so that I can fire most of the explosive charges at the same time. I used two flashlight batteries and some wire I ripped out of the instrument panel. The charges were all C-4. They'd just burn if we didn't give them an extra kick. Just say the word."

"Let's see if these guys coming are looking for us. Maybe they'll just walk on by."

"You don't really think that, do you?"

"Of course not, but it doesn't hurt to hope for the best."

The sudden burst of firing from a couple of AKs interrupted them. Gerber couldn't see anything through the trees. To Smith he said, "Get ready to blow the plane."

Now Gerber crawled toward the sound, remember-

ing that Custer's battle plan had always been to ride
to the sound of the shooting. Then he remembered
that Custer had been killed following his battle plan.

One of the Tais ran past him. Gerber could see the
man was bleeding from a minor cut on his head. The
volume of the firing increased.

Ahead of him, he could see an NVA soldier standing by a tree, just hosing down the area. Gerber
sighted and pulled the trigger of his weapon. The
enemy soldier looked amazed, staggered back two
steps, and fell, blood erupting from his chest.

Gerber moved around a tree and searched the jungle in front of him. He couldn't see anyone. He tried
to spot the flashes of the weapons, or even smoke
from them, but couldn't see that either. He pulled
back, toward the crash site, looking for Fetterman
and Tyme.

Bocker had found a good hiding place and was
lying among the bushes, just waiting. One of the
NVA soldiers was trying to pass him, unaware that
he was there. Bocker reached out, grabbed the man's
ankle. When he fell, Bocker knifed him.

Fetterman, at the first shot, had moved back to the
aircraft so that he could cover Smith. He situated
himself so that he could also see Jessup and Wilson.
Wilson was kneeling near a bush searching for someone to shoot at. Jessup was at his side but showed no
interest in shooting or being shot at.

Fetterman saw two of the NVA soldiers trying to
flank Wilson and Jessup. He ran toward them, dropped
to the ground, and waited for the enemy to show
themselves again. When they did, he fired a five-shot
burst that killed them both. He then leaped to his feet

and ran to Jessup, making him get down behind a fallen tree for added protection.

From the front, there was a shout, some wild firing, and the other two Tai guides ran back. One of them was shot, and pitched, headfirst, to the ground. The other was hit in the shoulder but didn't stop running.

McMillan saw this and left his position. Angling at the fleeing Tai, he cut off his retreat and tackled him. The wounded man rolled to his back, staring up at McMillan, the fear evident in his wide-open eyes.

McMillan opened his bag and dug through it. He was looking for one of the pressure bandages and was trying to calm the man. "Take it easy. You'll be okay," he told him.

He shook out the bandage and reached down. The shooting was still going on, as McMillan worked on the tribesmen. He thought that he should try to get him to cover, and as he thought of it, he felt a sudden burning, flaring pain in his back. He reached around as if to brush it off, wondering if he had been stung by one of the poisonous insects in the North Vietnamese jungle.

Around him, the green blurred into gray and black, and he felt suddenly dizzy. He dropped the bandage onto the man's stomach, rocked back on his heels, and then toppled over, trying to figure out what was happening. He lay there for a minute, almost unable to move, the sounds of the shooting fading.

The fighting between the two small forces fluctuated back and forth, and suddenly, Gerber found himself behind the enemy. He could see three of them trying to advance onto the crash site. He stood, braced his weapon against his hip, and fired, using the whole magazine. All three of the enemy dropped. Gerber could tell from the way they went down that they were dead.

He stripped the magazine from his weapon and threw it down, pulling another from his belt. He jammed the new magazine in, jacked the bolt back, let it slam home, and moved toward the crash site.

Tyme had curiously missed most of the fighting. He had been near the tail section of the airplane and could hear the shooting around him, but couldn't see the enemy. He stepped back, away from the airplane, and saw one of the Tais run.

Tyme moved forward then, trying to find where the Tai had been so that he could fill in the hole in the line. Still, he didn't see the enemy. He turned, looked toward the aircraft, and saw McMillan lying on the ground.

He got to his feet, ran to McMillan, and saw the blood that had pooled under him. Tyme grabbed him under the arms and dragged him to the rear of the U-2 where he would have some protection. He had almost been afraid to move McMillan, remembering that moving the injured sometimes compounded the injuries, but the danger of him being hit again made it imperative.

Now he could see some of the enemy running around in the trees. Tyme, firing the RPD in short bursts, killed two and wounded two more. He stayed where he was, trying to protect McMillan but didn't have the time to treat his wound.

The firing tapered off until it was sporadic—men shooting only when there was a target. Each side was maneuvering for position, not knowing exactly how large the opposition was.

Gerber ran out of the trees and found Smith crouched near the nose of the U-2. He was about to tell him to blow up the plane when he saw Tyme and McMillan. He ran to the rear, saw the wound, and said, "Can we move him?"

"I don't know. It seems to be a clean wound and isn't bleeding too much."

"Get Jessup and Wilson back here. I think we had better break contact and blow up the plane."

"Yes sir," said Tyme. He ran into the trees and found Fetterman still watching over the other two. He said, "Captain wants you all at the airplane."

When they got back, Gerber said, "Here's the deal. We've got to get out of here. If you guys will carry McMillan, we can blow the plane and leave. I'll stay back, with Smith and Tyme and you, Fetterman, fighting a holding action while Jessup, Wilson, and McMillan, with Bocker and Bao, head toward the east."

"Is it a good idea to split up your force like that, Captain?" Wilson asked.

"I'm not splitting the force. I'm trying to break contact before someone else gets shot and we can't get out of here. Tony, you get Bocker and Bao back here."

Fetterman got to his feet and headed into the jungle. A moment later, he reappeared, firing into the trees as he backed up slowly. Bocker and Bao were with him.

Once he was out of the trees, Fetterman took a couple of grenades and threw them. Bocker followed suit. The explosions silenced the chattering automatic rifles for a moment.

Using a poncho as a stretcher, Jessup and Wilson disappeared into the trees with McMillan. Bocker was right behind them. Bao had protested, but not much. He ran ahead of them, finding the path that would take them east with the least possible delay.

With them gone, Gerber had the others fall back, taking an ambush position just inside the trees. Smith stayed near the crash site only long enough to yank the string that would pull the pin of the smoke grenade he had set at the front of the trail of jet fuel. That done, he ran toward the others as the fuel caught fire, and with a red-hot whoosh, flames raced along the fuselage. Smith dropped to the ground long enough to touch the ends of the two wires to a pair of flashlight batteries clenched in his left hand. There was a series of small explosions as the black boxes and secret equipment blew up, throwing flaming pieces all over the tiny clearing. In seconds, the whole area was blazing, the flames leaping up to singe the palm leaves on the tallest trees and marking the destroyed aircraft's burning remains with a dirty, oily, black smoke.

Gerber signaled the men, and as one, they fell back, away from the crash site. They spread out, found hiding places, and waited for the pursuit.

The enemy rushed the burning plane. The heat drove them back and they realized that there was nothing there for them. They circled around, trying to find the trail of those who had been there.

They found the path and started down it. Gerber

saw them, let them get close, and then tossed a single grenade.

The enemy heard it fall among them and dived for cover. The explosion killed two of them and wounded a couple more. They opened fire blindly, shooting into the trees.

Gerber responded, raking the trail with his AK-47. He fired short bursts until the magazine was empty. He switched again and realized that there was now no return fire. He saw Fetterman using his silenced Swedish K. The others were not shooting.

He signaled Fetterman to fall back and to pass the word. The Green Berets broke contact, just as the VC did in South Vietnam. They left the NVA soldiers hiding near the trail, trying to figure out what to do next.

Fetterman ran ahead, taking the point position. Tyme backed him up, with Smith and Gerber covering the rear. Smith had grabbed an AK from a dead soldier so that he was carrying two of them. He caught up to Gerber and said, "Should we boobytrap the trail."

Continuing to move, Gerber said, "What do you have in mind?"

"I could rig one of the AKs so that it would fire down the trail if someone hit the trip wire. Might slow the pursuit. Takes a little longer to rig than a grenade, and might not kill anybody, but it produces a good psychological effect."

"How long would it take?"

"Five minutes."

"Okay. Stop to set it up. I'll catch Fetterman and

tell him to hold it up. We'll wait for you about a hundred meters down the trail.''

When Gerber trotted ahead, Smith stopped and checked the trees around him. He found one with a forked branch about four feet off the ground. He lashed the AK to one of the branches with a thin wire so that the barrel pointed down the trail, toward the enemy. He tied a slipknot with another wire in one end so that it was holding the trigger and the trigger guard. He pulled it back so that it was wrapped once around the pistol grip of the AK, pulled it down and under a thin branch near the ground. He crossed the trail and anchored the wire to a tree on that side. Now, if someone kicked the wire, it would be jerked forward, tighting the slipknot and pulling the trigger. With the weapon securely tied to the tree, it would put thirty rounds of 7.62mm ammunition down the trail. It could temporarily stop the pursuit and, with luck, kill a couple of the enemy.

Smith stepped over his wire, looked at the weapon, and checked the aim. That all done, he moved about twenty meters, took a grenade, and set it up along the trail. He bent the edges of the pin back so that it would release easily. He tied it to a tree so that the blast would be angled at the trail. By tying it, he knew that he would lose some of the fragmentation effect, but didn't have any other way of setting the trap quickly.

Two minutes later, he came up to Gerber and the rest of the men. They waited for a few seconds, listening, but didn't hear either of the traps go off. But then, they didn't hear any sounds from the enemy either.

Just before they moved out, Smith said, ''You

know, if we take a couple of minutes here, we could build another trap.''

''What do you need?''

''We set a grenade up so that it falls into the center of the trail. It doesn't even have to go off. The enemy, seeing that, dives to the sides, and lands on some of the pungi stakes that we could hide there.''

Gerber whipped out his knife, hacked off a branch from a sapling, and started sharpening it. The others followed suit. They planted the stakes on the side of the trail while Smith rigged the grenade.

Twenty minutes later, as they ran down the trail, they heard a long burst from an AK. Smith said, ''They've reached the first boobytrap.''

There was more shooting then, as the NVA tried to wipe out the Americans who were no longer there. Apparently, after the brief phony firefight, they charged forward, because there was an explosion as they hit the second trap. Firing erupted all over again, as the NVA shot wildly into the bushes, not sure of what was happening.

Still running, Gerber caught up with Smith and said, ''You got any more ideas?''

''I have lots of them, Captain, but I don't have the equipment I need.''

''Aren't you the one who told me that there was always something else to be done?''

''Well, I could set up another grenade trap. Lead guy would trip it and the men at the rear would get it.''

''How?''

''Easy,'' panted Smith. ''Just set it up so that the trip wire is ten or twelve meters long.''

*　　*　　*

Smith stopped to set up the trap, while the others waited, watching and listening. But now the pursuit was so far behind them that there was no sound from it. Gerber didn't know if they had given up, were resting, or were all dead or wounded.

An hour later, still having heard nothing from the NVA or seen any units looking for them, they caught up with Bocker and his party.

CHAPTER 10_____

"How's he doing?" asked Gerber.

Bocker stared for a moment at McMillan. "I wish I knew, sir. I've got the bleeding pretty well controlled, I think, but he could be hemorrhaging internally. He keeps drifting in and out of consciousness. The round was slowed down some when it went through his pack, but it's still deep enough that I couldn't find the bullet. He might be okay if we can get him some medical attention fairly soon, but out here . . ."

He left the sentence unfinished.

Gerber understood the problem. All the Special Forces men had received combat medical training beyond the emergency first-aid taught to a regular infantry soldier, but they were still less qualified than a medic or hospital corpsman. McMillan had been the only medical specialist on the mission. His normal assistant, Staff Sergeant Washington, was in a Saigon hospital recuperating from wounds received during the VC attack on Special Forces Camp A-555.

Now McMillan himself had been wounded, and the others could do little more than apply first-aid and curse their own insufficient knowledge. One thing was certain: even if the bleeding was stopped, McMillan could still die from infection without proper medical treatment. In the tropical environment of the Mekong Delta, infection could advance beyond the point of treatable in a few hours from a particularly dirty wound. Here, in the subtropical north, the time factor would probably be extended somewhat. How long, Gerber didn't know.

"Okay, we'll rest for fifteen minutes, then go on," he said. "Tyme, Smith, security front and rear. Master Sergeant!"

"Right here, sir," said Fetterman.

"Drop back half a klick or so and make sure our trail is clear. Don't loiter, just make a quick check, then get back here."

"Yes sir."

Fetterman moved off quickly, back down the trail, and Gerber sank down to eat one of the West German C-rations. The main course was an unidentified red meat that tasted suspiciously like horse flesh but was otherwise unremarkable. Gerber reflected wryly that it was, at least, twice as good as the ham and lima beans found in American rations. He polished off this gastronomic delight with some sort of wafer that he used to scrape applesauce out of a tiny can and washed it all down with a small can of something that might have been apple juice. The juice, he decided, was definitely the best part of the cuisine, which led him to the observation that combat meals were pretty much the same the world over. He was in the process of giving the remains of the meal a decent burial when Fetterman and Smith came hurrying up.

"We got company again, Captain," Fetterman reported. "I figure about twenty-five, maybe thirty minutes behind us. They're moving slow, but they're staying right on our trail. I think all the boobytraps we've been leaving are making them cautious, but they've got a couple of damned good trackers."

"Trackers? Damn! Are you sure?"

The master sergeant nodded vigorously.

"How many?"

"Two trackers out front. About two dozen guys following. They got some officer leading them."

"How do you know?"

"Khaki uniform, Sam Browne belt, binoculars hung around his neck."

"Right. Well, we're going to have to lose them. Sully, you got any ideas for getting those trackers off our tail?"

"I'm starting to run kind of low on ideas, sir. I suppose we could leave Sergeant McMillan's pack where they could find it."

"That's kind of obvious, isn't it, Sully? Don't you think these guys might be a bit too bright for that? Especially after the way you've been educating them."

"I'm counting on that, sir. I'll run a trip from the pack to a smoke grenade, which they'll find, but won't know what it is. Then I'll put a willy pete under the pack."

"Not bad. But if you thought of it, they might too."

Smith grinned. "I'm also counting on that. I put a pressure release trigger under the grenade, with a four-second delay. The release activates a non-electric blasting cap, taped to a piece of det-cord. The det-cord has another cap on the far end, with a claymore on the end of that. I'll need about fifteen minutes to rig it.''

''What's the four-second delay for?'' asked Fetterman.

''To give everybody time to stand back up, once they think they've disarmed the grenade under the pack.''

''You've got twelve minutes,'' said Gerber. ''Do it.''

Half an hour later, Fetterman once again rejoined the rest of the patrol. ''It didn't work,'' he said.

''What the hell do you mean, it didn't work?'' said Smith. ''They couldn't have missed it. I left the pack right in the middle of the road.''

''They didn't miss it. They didn't touch it either. They just walked around it. One of the guys wanted to check it out, but the officer wouldn't let thim.''

''Damn!'' said Smith. ''Who are those guys?''

''Don't take it so hard, Sully,'' Gerber consoled him. ''They'll be back for it.''

''Captain,'' said Tyme, ''shouldn't we make like a shepherd and get the flock out of here?''

''I'm ready to go,'' said Jessup.

Gerber shot him a glance and turned to Fetterman. ''Master Sergeant, take the point.''

''Thanks, sir, I was getting kind of tired of bringing up the rear.''

''The rest of you get ready,'' said Gerber. ''We move out in three minutes.''

Jessup nudged Wilson. "I'm not waiting for these clowns. We hang around here, that NVA patrol is going to catch us. And I've already been caught once."

He took off down the trail before Wilson could stop him.

"Where's that jerkoff going?" called Gerber, pointing at the hastily retreating back of Jessup.

"I couldn't stop him, Captain," said Wilson.

"Tyme, go get that idiot and bring his head back here."

Tyme ran after the fleeing pilot. Two hundred yards down the trail he came to a fork. "Now which way did the dumb bastard go?" He examined the trail, noticed that the leaves of some of the lower plants had bent to one side, and ran up the trail to the right.

A few seconds later, Tyme caught sight of Jessup crashing loudly through the brush fifty yards ahead of him. "Jessup, you asshole, you're going the wrong way."

Jessup turned to yell over his shoulder at Tyme and tripped over a low object lying across the trail. He hit the ground hard, rolled once, and was still.

The object immediately reared up, staring Tyme in the face. It was a king cobra. It must have been eighteen feet long. And it was not amused.

Tyme slid to a halt fifteen yards from the snake. "Ho-ly shit!" He called to Jessup: "Don't move! I'll kill it . . . I hope."

Tyme sighted carefully and squeezed off a short burst from his submachine gun.

The snake jerked backward as if thrown, and crashed

onto the trail. It thrashed about noisely, reared again, and rushed straight for Tyme. Clearly, the cobra was not amused. Tyme was not amused.

The Green Beret sergeant fired again, emptying his weapon into the snake, shredding it. Little bits and pieces of its flesh flew through the air, splattering the bushes with reptilian blood. The snake's body smashed into the trunk of a teak tree and fell heavily to the ground. This time it did not move.

"Okay, you can get up now."

"No, I can't," said Jessup, his voice furred with pain.

"What the hell do you mean that you can't? Those things usually travel in pairs, and I don't want to be around when the other shows up, in case we just killed its little brother."

"Well then help me. I can't move."

Tyme, reloading his weapon, walked forward. Jessup was lying on his back in the grass, with small chunks of snake all over him. He was covered in blood. "Are you hit?"

"I don't think so. It's my back. I heard something snap when I fell."

Tyme, fearing a severed spine, warned, "Don't move then. I'll get help."

"What about the other snake?"

"You better pray I was wrong about them traveling in pairs. Otherwise you're going to have a lot of explaining to do."

Tyme was back in two minutes with the rest of the main group.

Bocker crouched over the prostrate Jessup and said, "My professional medical opinion is that he fucked up his back. I don't know what I can do about it.''

"Just one more thing to go wrong," said Gerber. "McMillan said it was a possibility. Can we move him?"

"Can you move your legs?" asked Bocker.

"Yes, but it hurts. I don't think I can walk."

Bocker shrugged. "Seems to me we have no choice. We have to move him."

"Okay," said Gerber, "You and Tyme cut some poles and I'll get a poncho."

Fetterman appeared out of nowhere. "What the fuck are you people doing here?"

Quickly, Gerber told the master sergeant what had happened. He concluded, saying, "Of all the lousy luck. I don't see how things could get any worse."

"Come with me, Captain, and I'll show you. There's a T-54 sitting on the beach."

"A T-54?" said Gerber. "What's a T-54 doing sitting on the beach?"

"Sunbathing, I imagine. Either that or waiting to blow those SWIFT boats out of the water."

"I don't fucking believe it. How could they know? Who are those guys?"

"Whatever we're going to do about that T-54, we better do it fast, sir. We've still got company coming behind us."

Gerber turned to Bocker. "Get on the radio and see if the SWIFT boats are close and see if they've got any ideas."

The radio wouldn't work.

"How about the walkie-talkie?" Gerber asked Bocker.

"Battery's dead in that, sir."

Tyme said, "Maybe we ought to just surrender."

Gerber shot him an icy glare and then smiled. "Maybe you're right."

Both men grinned.

"Well, Sergeant Bocker," said Gerber, "I'd say you better get busy and fix that damned radio or we're going to be in deep kemchi."

Bocker tore frantically into the radio, looking for something he could fix. In two minutes he looked up. "Sir, the problem's with the antenna connection. I think maybe I can make this thing work if we can rig a field expedient antenna."

"You mean just hang a wire from a tree?"

"Well, more or less, sir. The problem is that I don't have any wire."

"How about some of Smith's lead wire for the demolitions?"

"Hadn't thought of that," said Bocker. "It'd be the wrong size. Guess that's why I didn't think of it."

"Can't you trim it down, or something?"

"It's worth a try, considering the alternative."

Gerber turned to Smith. "Sully, we've got to do something about those guys behind us. If you've got any dirty tricks left, now is the time to use them. And I mean use all of them. Take Fetterman and Tyme with you, set as many traps as you can. Start about five hundred meters down the trail and work your way in this direction. Don't take too long, though. I'll stand here and utter words of encouragement at Sergeant Bocker."

*   *   *

Twenty minutes later, Gerber said to Bocker, "Well, Sergeant. It's about that time. Are you going to get any noise out of that thing or are we going to have to start growing gills?"

Bocker shrugged and tried the handset of the radio again. It was the third antenna setup he had tried. A look of amazement spread across his face and he held the handset out to Gerber. "It's the boats. They want to talk to you."

"Beachrunner. Beachrunner. This is Pack Rat. Over."

"Pack Rat. This is Beachrunner. We are ready to extract. Say condition of beach. Over."

"Roger, Beachrunner. Be advised that there are tanks, one, on the beach. Over."

"Roger. Understand tanks, one, on the beach. Will extract as soon as you eliminate the tank. Over."

Gerber exploded. "Christ! They expect us to do everything. Galvin, we got any anti-armor for the RPG?"

"We had two. Smith took them."

At that moment the jungle was shattered by two explosions. "Sounds like he ain't bringing them back either."

"Goddamm it!" swore Gerber. He tried the radio again. "Beachrunner. Beachrunner. This is Pack Rat. We no longer have means to neutralize tank. Can you handle? Over."

"A fucking tank? You've got to be kidding. The biggest thing we've got is a .50-cal."

"Well, mister, that's a damn sight bigger than anything we've got."

"But it's you who wants off the beach."

"Roger! Pick us up in fifteen minutes. We'll take care of it." Gerber threw the handset at the radio. "Bocker, take that thing out and shoot it."

There was another loud explosion, followed by sustained firing. A few moments later, Smith, Tyme, and Fetterman burst onto the trail.

"They're five minutes behind us now, sir," Fetterman said.

A series of sharp explosions interrupted him. Fetterman looked in that direction and then said, "Make that four minutes."

"Gentleman," said Gerber, "we have a serious problem. The SWIFT boats won't be here for fifteen minutes, and they won't be here at all unless we can take care of the tank."

Fetterman said, "We better hurry."

"Sorry, Sully. Wish I hadn't told you to use everything now," said Gerber. "We could use some of it back. Especially those two RPG rounds."

"Gee, I'm sorry about that too, sir. Real sorry." Smith dug around in his rucksack and came up with a two-pound lump of plastic explosive. "Looks like this is the last of my bag of tricks."

"I thought you used everything," said Gerber.

"I try never to do that," said Smith. "Always figure that there is one more thing that needs to be blown up."

"Okay," said Gerber. "We've got a couple of grenades, some small arms, and one block of C-4. Master Sergeant, what's the best way to knock out a T-54?"

"I'd recommend a 155mm howitzer, or a B-52 strike, sir. Since we don't have ready access to either of those, I'd recommend that we take Sergeant Smith's plastic explosive and put it under the turret on the right side.''

''That means crawling between the treads.''

''Yes sir. Exactly.''

''I guess you know who the smallest man here is.''

''Yes sir. Figure I'll make the smallest spot on the sand when the tank runs over me.''

''I was hoping you'd be quick enough to get out of the way before that happens. We'll provide cover for you. From both directions.'' Gerber looked at Wilson. ''You'll have to stay here to protect Jessup and McMillan. As soon as we've eliminated the tank, we'll come back for you.''

''And if the tank takes care of you?''

''I would suggest that you fade into the jungle and practice becoming a tree.''

Fetterman took the block of plastic from Smith. The demolitions sergeant had already fitted it with a detonator with a five-second fuse.

Gerber deployed his men in a small thicket just where the trail forked. The front of the thicket opened onto a low ridge overlooking the beach. The rear faced back up the main trail, down which the NVA would have to come. Below and to the left, Gerber could see Fetterman crawling through sand behind the T-54 tank. Except for a slight depression in the sand, there was no cover at all.

''Even if only one of those guys turns around,'' whispered Tyme, ''he's dead.''

''If only one of those guys turns around, Sergeant, we'll all be dead.''

Behind them, another string of Smith's boobytraps went off. Gerber wondered how many minutes away Fetterman would have guessed they were now.

The tank was sitting still on the beach. Its hatches were closed and its main gun was pointing out to sea. Its engine was off. It appeared to be calmly waiting for the boats.

Fetterman crawled up to the back of the tank and disappeared beneath it. Fifteen seconds later, he crawled back out from underneath it, rose calmly to his feet, and casually walked away.

Gerber said, "What the hell is going on?"

The last string of explosions had sounded ominously close and Wilson had still heard nothing from the beach. It was becoming clear to him that the NVA would arrive long before the SWIFT boats, whether Gerber's men were successful in dealing with the tank or not.

He had come on this mission for one reason alone: to get the film out. Rescuing Senator Jessup's son meant nothing to him. That was merely an extraneous personal matter. But for Wilson, the mission always took precedence over personal considerations, and it looked to him as though he was going to have to do something about it himself if this mission were to have any chance for success.

He took the film canister from the U-2 out of his pack and handed it to Jessup. He didn't trust the dandified, playboy pilot, but Gerber wasn't there.

"Look, Jessup, I want you to make sure this gets aboard the ship. That's all you've got to do from here on out. Make sure that this gets aboard the ship.

Once you're aboard ship, give it to Gerber. He'll see to it that it gets to the right place.''

''What about my control officer?''

''Negative. There isn't time for that. This stuff has got to get to Langley immediately. Besides, you'll be too busy getting pats on the back from your father and his congressional cronies.''

''You know about my father?''

''If we'd known you didn't have the film, why do you think we'd have bothered with you? We could have gone straight for the plane. If your old man wasn't a member of the Senate Intelligence Committee, you might still be entertaining the guards back at that NVA camp.''

''But you needed me to find the plane.''

''No. We needed the tribesmen. You didn't find shit for us. But we couldn't be sure of getting the political cooperation we needed to authorize this mission unless we got you out for your old man. He's got the President's ear. Looks like your daddy's still paying the bills. Now I guess it's time for me to go pay mine.''

''What are you going to do?'' asked Jessup.

''I'm going to see if I can't slow that NVA patrol up a bit more so that Gerber and his men will have time to get you and the film out of here. Make sure that the film gets on board. Without the film, we didn't need this mission and that means we didn't need you.''

He handed Jessup an AK-47, picked up his own, and checked to make sure that it was fully loaded. Then he checked McMillan's gear, took what grenades and ammunition the man had left. As an afterthought, he picked up the walkie-talkie, not realizing that the battery was dead.

"Wilson," said Jessup. "I don't understand why you're doing this. Why are you throwing your life away?"

The CIA man looked down at him, knowing that when the NVA got there the whole team would be killed, the film would be lost, and the mission would be an entire write-off. "Jessup, you asshole," he said. "You just never will understand, will you? That's life, man. It's a dirty job but somebody's got to do it."

He turned his back and disappeared down the trail.

Before he reached the fork, Wilson left the trail and moved directly through the jungle until he crossed the main trail. He found a small, natural depression beneath the roots of a large, hardwood tree. He didn't know much about the tactics of jungle fighting, but it looked like the most defensible place. He arranged his grenades and magazines in front of him. There were four magazines and three grenades.

He had by now learned enough about jungle fighting to know that he was outclassed. It was unlikely that he would ever hear the approaching enemy. The plan was simple. He would wait until the main body of troops came by and open fire.

He only had to wait two minutes. He let the first two men go by. He remembered vaguely from his training at Camp Perry that you were supposed to do that. When a group of seven walked past his position, he pulled the pin of a grenade, threw it onto the trail, and opened fire.

Wilson almost forgot to duck when the grenade went off. As shrapnel whined passed his head, he pulled the pin on the second grenade and held it ready. As soon as it was safe, he threw the grenade into the middle of the trail and resumed firing.

Almost immediately, the rear of the NVA element began a flanking maneuver. Despite the fact that his position came under heavy fire at once, Wilson was able to hold up the NVA patrol for almost five minutes, using his last grenade and nearly all of his ammunition in the process.

Finally the NVA worked themselves close enough to Wilson's position to throw grenades at him. Wilson had always thought that the movie heroes who threw themselves on grenades were being a bit silly. He preferred to throw them back. It worked fine until the NVA figured out what he was doing.

As the AK-47's bolt locked back, indicating that Wilson had fired his final round, an NVA stick grenade exploded immediately in front of his tree, the impact knocking him momentarily unconscious.

Two NVA soldiers came over to check the body and take trophies. Wilson was dimly aware of their hands on his body. One of them was trying to pull off his boots.

Someone barked an order in Vietnamese, and the two men stopped pulling at his clothing. As one of them turned him over, Wilson drew the combat knife from his belt and drove it between the man's ribs. The other soldier seemed too startled to react.

The last thing Wilson saw was the man who had given the order to stop stripping him. He was dressed in the uniform of a communist Chinese major. He had a small pistol in his hand. With it he shot Wilson once in the face.

Wilson died not knowing that he had killed six of the enemy and wounded two more. He had held the patrol up for nearly eight minutes.

Fetterman stood at the edge of the beach and cupped his hands together in order to shout to Gerber up on the ridge above. "It's empty."

Gerber looked at Tyme. "What did he say?"

"I don't know. It sounded like he said it was empty."

Gerber yelled back down to the beach. "What did you say?"

"I said, the fucking thing is empty. It's a derelict. There's nobody in it. It's nothing but a rusted-out piece of junk."

"Where's the crew?"

"How the hell should I know? Maybe in fucking Hanoi. It doesn't look like they've been here since the French pulled out."

"Well, I'll be damned," said Gerber. He yelled back at Fetterman, "Secure the beach. We'll be right down."

He nudged Tyme. "Come on, let's get the wounded. Bocker, tell them to get that frigging boat in here."

As they reached the wounded, heavy firing broke out on the main trail. Gerber glanced at the two men on the stretchers. McMillan was still unconscious.

"Where's Wilson?" Gerber demanded of Jessup.

"Went off to be a fucking hero."

"What's that supposed to mean?"

"He figured somebody had to hold up the NVA patrol or you guys wouldn't have time enough to get the tank. So he appointed himself."

"What'll we do?" said Tyme.

"There's nothing we can do. The man made his decision."

"Does that mean we're ready to go?" asked Jessup.

In the distance the firing had become a full-scale battle.

"Tyme, stay here with Jessup. We'll carry McMillan to the beach and send Bocker back to help you."

"Aren't you going to call Wilson and tell him we're ready to go," said Jessup. "He took the walkie-talkie."

"It doesn't work."

"He didn't know that."

"Of course, he didn't know that. If he had, he wouldn't have taken the worthless piece of junk with him. We'll wait for him on the beach as long as we can. That's all we can do."

From the intensity of the firing, Gerber knew that Wilson was already dead. It would make no sense to get the rest of them killed trying to retrieve his body.

Gerber and Smith picked up the stretcher with McMillan on it and headed for the beach. As they passed Bocker, Gerber said to him, "Galvin, those damned navy boys better be coming in. Did you talk to them?"

"Yes sir, the boats are on the way. They seemed real impressed when I told them we'd neutralized the tank."

"Bao, you come on with us. We're going to the beach. Bocker, you let the navy know that we're

going to lose our communications and then go back
and give Tyme a hand with Jessup.''

Bocker looked suprised. ''What about Wilson?''

''I don't think Mr. Wilson is going to make it.''

The two navy SWIFT boats pulled into the shallows,
and the Green Berets splashed aboard, holding the
stretchers on their shoulders to keep Jessup and Mc-
Millan dry.

Gerber found the captain of the tiny vessel and
persuaded him to wait as long as possible.

''I've still one man ashore,'' he said.

The wait lasted all of forty-five seconds. The NVA
patrol swarmed onto the ridge overlooking the beach.
The entire treeline seemed to blaze with muzzle flashes.

''Sorry, Captain,'' said the navy man. ''Looks like
time just ran out for your boy.''

As the SWIFT boats reversed away from the beach,
their gunners opened fire on the NVA, raking the
edge of the forest with .50-cal machine-gun slugs,
chopping down several small trees, and decimating
the enemy.

''Captain,'' said one of the navy men.

''What is it, Corpsman?'' said the SWIFT boat
commander.

''I think the other guy is going to be okay. But I'm
sorry, sir, this man's dead.''

Gerber felt the blood drain from his face. He
pushed his way to the front of the boat and knelt
down by McMillan. ''He's not dead. He's still
breathing.''

''No sir,'' said the corpsman. ''The other guy.
The one shot in the side.''

"Side? What are you talking about?"

"This man here. Looks like the bullet went through both lungs and the heart."

Gerber stared down at Jessup. "He had a back injury," he said. "He wasn't hit."

"Must have been a stray round from the beach," said the corpsman. "We've got four or five holes in the cabin." The corpsman proudly pointed to the combat damage.

Gerber stared for a moment at the holes, then looked down at Jessup again. The film canister from the plane was clenched in his hands.

A petty officer stuck his helmeted head up through the hatchway of the tiny bullet-riddled cabin. "Captain," he said to the skipper, "we got a boatload of trouble. Three of them in fact. And they're headed our way. Fast. Looks like Russian-made PTs."

"We sure don't want to hang around for those guys. They'll have us outgunned. Helmsman, come about to course one-one-zero degrees. Full speed for the *Maddox*."

CHAPTER 11 _____

Lieutenant Colonel Alan Bates and Captain Mack Gerber sat drinking quietly at an isolated table across the floor from the makeshift stage and concert hall speakers in the officers' club at Ton Son Nhut. A half-empty bottle of Beam's Choice sat between them. It was the second bottle Bates had bought that evening. It probably wouldn't be the last.

"Have you talked to Karen?" Bates asked gently.

"No," said Gerber. "I haven't called her yet. I need some time to sort things out."

"You both still have some leave coming. I could arrange for you to have it together."

Gerber smiled weakly. "Isn't this where I came in? No, not just yet, Colonel. Maybe in a day or two."

"Look, Mack. You can't be so hard on yourself. You were given a damn near impossible job to do, and you did it. And you did it without losing anyone on your team."

207

"I lost Jessup and Wilson."

"I meant on the A Detachment. By the way, how's McMillan doing? Have you seen him?"

Gerber shook his head. "Tried to but they wouldn't let me in. All I know is his condition is listed as stable, whatever that means."

"And how about Lieutenant Bao?"

"Leg's going to be okay. Doctors here were impressed with the makeshift cast McMillan came up with."

Bates waved at the bartender, and when he had his attention said, "What time is the President's speech?"

"In about thirty minutes, Colonel. Don't worry, we'll pipe through the whole club."

"Johnson talking tonight?" asked Gerber. "What's this one about?"

Bates shrugged. "Rumor is that it is some kind of major policy address. Not being part of the cabinet, I don't usually get an advanced copy of the text." He grinned lopsidedly and poured each of them another drink.

Gerber shook his head. "Two men dead, another maybe dying, another man hurt, and all we've got to show for it is a damned piece of film. I hope the pictures are worth it."

"I didn't want to tell you this, but I guess I'd rather have you find out from me than from someone else. Langley said that the film canister had cracked. The film was useless. There are no pictures."

Gerber gave Bates a hard look. "Well, shit, the perfect end to a positively wonderful mission. Wait a minute, I'm not that drunk yet. That film canister was intact when I handed it over to the CIA. Maybe not perfect condition, but it damn sure didn't have any holes in it.''

"Does it matter?" said Bates. "Their story is that it was cracked. If that's what they want to tell us, fine. You didn't really expect them to let us know what was really on the film, did you?''

"I guess not," said Gerber. "I just don't like being lied to, especially when it's such an obvious lie. At least, I hope it is. I'd hate to think we really did do all that for nothing. Oh hell, at least I'm convinced the product was in reasonably good shape when we handed it over. If they fucked it up afterward, I guess that's their problem.''

Bates felt it best to change the topic. "What's the rest of your team doing tonight?''

"I would imagine they're over at the NCO club doing the same thing we are.''

Bates drained his glass, poured himself another shot, and said, "You better hurry. You're falling behind.''

Gerber pulled a full bottle out of his shirt, set it on the table, and said, "Slow and steady wins the race.''

"I like the way you drink. Have we ever been drunk together before?''

"Not that I can remember, Colonel. Besides, I usually don't waste all this good alcohol on a man.''

"Well, there has to be a first time for everything. Well, almost everything.''

There was a sudden commotion at the door of the club. A number of field grade officers and a couple of State Department people Bates recognized from the U.S. embassy thundered into the room like an invading horde. Most were quite drunk. A few were extremely drunk.

One of the diplomatic personnel pumped on the bar with his doubled fist and whistled loudly until it was quiet. "Have you people heard what ole beagle ears did?"

"Sir," said the bartender, "the President is about to speak. Would you please find a seat and be quiet."

"That's what I'm talking about, you silly little man. The President's speech. Ole beagle ears has gone and got us into a full-scale war. A real live shooting match."

A colonel took the man by an arm and guided him toward a table. "Gary, you're going to have to quiet down or we're all going to get thrown out of here."

Over the speakers, they all heard the booming voice of the announcer. "Ladies and gentlemen, the President of the United States."

My fellow Americans. As president and commander-in-chief, it is my duty to the American people to report that renewed hostile actions against United States ships on the high seas in the Gulf of Tonkin have today required me to order the military forces of the United States to take action in reply.

Somebody at the bar groaned, "Oh shit!"

The initial attack on the destroyer Maddox, *on August 2, was repeated today by a number of hostile vessels attacking two U.S. destroyers with torpedoes. The destroyers and supporting aircraft acted at once on the orders I gave after the initial act of aggression. We believe at least two of the attacking boats were sunk. There were no U.S. losses.*

Gerber stared dumbly at Bates. "The *Maddox*? He did say the *Maddox*, didn't he?"

The performance of commanders and crews in this engagement is in the highest tradition of the United States Navy. But repeated acts of violence against the armed forces of the United States must be met not only with alert defense but with positive reply. That reply is being given as I speak to you tonight. Air action is now in execution against gunboats and certain supporting facilities in North Vietnam which have been used in these hostile operations.

In the larger sense this new act of aggression, aimed directly at our own forces, again brings home to all of us in the United States the importance of the struggle for peace and security in Southeast Asia. Aggression by terror against the peaceful villagers of South Vietnam has now been joined by open aggression on the high seas against the United States of America.

"Positive reply? What's does he mean a positive reply?" the man at the bar asked no one in particular.

"It means he's starting a goddamned war, you asshole," the man named Gary shouted before his embassy friends could quiet him down.

The determination of all Americans to carry out our full commitment to the people and to the government of South Vietnam will be redoubled by this outrage. Yet our response, for the present, will be limited and fitting. We Americans know, although others appear to forget, the risks of spreading conflict. We still seek no wider war.

Gerber threw his glass at the wall. The glass shattered into a hundred tiny splinters. Gerber picked up the bottle, drank nearly half of the remaining liquor, and slammed the bottle back down on the tabletop. "Damn it, Colonel. He's talking about us. You know, he's talking about us."

"Take it easy, Mack. Let's hear the man out. He's not going to do something crazy like start a war."

I have instructed the Secretary of State to make this position totally clear to friends and to adversaries and, indeed, to all. I have instructed Ambassador Stevenson to raise this matter immediately and urgently before the Security Council of the United Nations. Finally, I have today met with the leaders of both parties in the Congress of the United States and I have informed them that I shall immediately request the Congress to pass a resolution making it clear that our government is united in its determination to take all necessary measures in support of freedom and in defense of peace in Southeast Asia.

Bates looked dumbfounded. "My God, I can't believe it. He's going to bomb the north. He has bombed the north! Doesn't the man realize what's going on over here? You don't keep a war limited by bombing Hanoi. You can't defend peace with a bomber."

I have been given encouraging assurance by these leaders of both parties that such a resolution will be promptly introduced, freely and expeditiously debated, and passed with overwhelming support. And just a few minutes ago I was able to reach Senator Goldwater, and I am glad to say that he has expressed his support of the statement that I am making to you tonight.

It is a solemn responsibility to have to order even

limited military action by forces whose overall strength is as vast and as awesome as those of the United States of America, but it is my considered conviction, shared throughout your government, that firmness in the right is indispensable today for peace, that firmness will always be measured. Its mission is peace.

Gerber, the blood drained from his face, looked at Bates. "My God, Colonel. What have we done?"

GLOSSARY

AK-47 - Assault rifle normally used by the North Vietnamese and the Viet Cong.

AO - Area of operations.

ARVN - Army of the Republic of Vietnam. A South Vietnamese soldier. Also known as Marvin Arvin.

ASAP - As soon as posible.

BODY COUNT - The number of enemy killed, wounded, or captured during an operation. Used by Saigon and Washington as a means of measuring progress of the war.

BOOM-BOOM - Term used by the Vietnamese prostitutes in selling their product.

C-130 - A four-engine cargo plane called the Hercules.

CHICOM - Chinese communist.

CLAYMORE - An antipersonnel mine that fires 750 steel balls with a lethal range of fifty meters.

COMPRESSOR STALL - Failure of the compressor in a jet engine.

DZ - Drop zone, for parachuting.

ECM - Electronic counter measures, jamming.

EEI - Essential elements of intelligence. Items on the ground that a pilot is to look for.

E-TOOL - An entrenching tool. A small folding shovel.

FIVE - Radio call sign for the executive officer of a unit.

FORWARD ROLL - A type of parachute landing.

G-FORCES - Force of gravity on the body caused by steep turns or acceleration.

GLIDE RATIO - Distance aircraft will glide after engine failure.

HALO - High-altitude, low-opening parachute drop.

HE - High-explosive ammunition.

HOOTCH - Almost any shelter, from temporary to long term.

LLDB - Luc-Luong Dac-Biet. The South Vietnamese Special Forces.

M-14 - Standard rifle of the U.S., eventually replaced by the M-16. It fired the standard NATO round: 7.62mm.

MACV - Military Assistance Command, Vietnam.

MEDEVAC - Also called dustoff: helicopter used to take the wounded to the medical facilities.

MONTAGNARD - A people inhabiting a highly montainous region, chiefly in southern Vietnam bordering on Cambodia.

NCO - A noncommissioned officer. A noncom. A sergeant.

NINETEEN - The average age of the combat soldier in Vietnam.

NOUC-MAM - A strong-smelling sauce, made from fish, used by the Vietnamese.

NUNG - An ethnic Tai subgroup whose men were famed for their prowess as warriors. They inhabited both North and South Vietnam.

OP - Observation post, operation.

PLF - Parachute landing fall.

PRC-10 - Man-portable radio.

PUNGI STAKE - Sharpened bamboo hidden to penetrate the foot, sometimes dipped in feces.

RPD - Soviet light machine gun 7.62mm.

RPG - Rocket-propelled grenade.

SHEAR LOAD - Stresses on the wings of an aircraft.

SHURIKEN - Oriental throwing star.

SIX - Radio call sign for the unit commander.

SKS - Soviet-made carbine.

SMG - Submachine gun.

TAI - A Vietnamese ethnic group living in the mountainous regions.

THREE - Radio call sign of the operations officer.

THE WORLD - The United States.

TOC - Tactical Operations Center.

U-2 - High-flying aircraft used for recon.

VC - Viet Cong, called Victor Charlie, or just Charlie.

VIET CONG - A contraction of Vietnam Cong San (Vietnamese communist).

VNAF - South Vietnamese air force.

WILLY PETE - WP, white phosphorus, called smoke rounds. Also used for casualty effect.

Watch for

CHOPPER COMMAND

next in THE SCORPION SQUAD
series from Pinnacle Books

coming in March!